FALLING FOR THE WINGMAN

The Kelly Brothers, Book 3

by

Crista McHugh

Falling for the Wingman
Copyright 2014 by Crista McHugh
Edited by Gwen Hayes
Copyedited by Elizabeth MS Flynn
Cover Art by Sweet N' Spicy Designs

ISBN-13: 978-1-940559-93-3

CHAPTER ONE

Sometimes four hundred and fifty horsepower wasn't enough.

Caleb Kelly rammed the clutch and shifted gears. The engine of his classic Baldwin Motion Camaro growled in response and accelerated along the two-lane highway in rural Alabama, but it still wasn't fast enough. He was already too late as it was, and every second that crept by felt like an eternity.

Kourtney had left him, and now he was chasing his last chance to win her back.

The ringing of his phone interrupted the Metallica blasting through the radio, and he clicked on the Bluetooth. "What?"

"I just got your message," Adam, the eldest brother in the family, said. "What happened?"

"I'm asking myself the same goddamn thing." The speedometer teetered on seventy, but he felt like he was crawling. "I came home expecting to find Kourtney there, and all I found was a note."

"She left you while you were deployed?"

"Yep." A beat-up Ford Taurus pulled out in front of him. Caleb slammed on the brakes to avoid hitting the car, but his heart kept pace with the RPMs of his engine.

1

"Did she give you any warning?"

"Nothing." He paused and recounted all the emails she'd sent him while he was gone. None of them seemed to indicate she was unhappy. Yes, they mentioned that she missed him, and some of the later ones indicated she was bored living in Ft. Walton without him, but none of them prepared him for the dust-covered letter that was waiting on his pillow when he came back from Afghanistan. "Until I walked through the door this afternoon, I expected her to be waiting for me."

Of course, his first warning should've been when he didn't spot her with the other families at the airfield.

"When did you last hear from her?"

"About a month ago. She didn't answer my last few emails, but I always wonder how much the DOD lets go through."

"What did her note say?"

Caleb tightened his jaw and drummed on the steering wheel. The driver in front of him seemed oblivious to his haste, cruising along the highway as part of a leisurely Sunday drive. "She said she wasn't cut out to be an Air Force girlfriend."

"She knew what she was getting into when she started dating you." A heavy sigh came from the other end. "Are you sure you want her back?"

Caleb ran his hand over the small metal bulge in his pocket. It was a small figurine of an angel made out of watch parts and other pieces of scrap metal. The halo was purposely crooked, and the wings appeared to be made from an antique Army Air Corps pilot badge. Kourtney had given it to him before he deployed, joking that it was a good luck charm. He'd carried it with him on every mission, and more than once, he'd escaped some tense situations without a scratch.

But it was more than the good luck charm. He'd been crazy about her before he left—as hot as she was, what man wouldn't be—but while he was away, he'd discovered a new side to her. Her emails revealed a woman of strength, patience, and hope that endeared her to his heart. When he was alone and cold and worried if he'd come out of the next mission alive, she'd always say something that would set his soul at ease. As his deployment came to closer to the end, so did his resolution to marry her.

"I doubt you'd understand, Adam."

"Try me. After all, I'm the first one of us getting married."

"If Ben doesn't beat you to it." The ribbing soothed some of Caleb's frustration, and a grin tugged at the corners of his mouth. Both of his older brothers had found women they couldn't live without. Now it was his turn. "Remember how I told you she was special before I left?"

"Yeah."

"Well, she's more than that. She kept me alive over there with her letters, and now I want to spend the rest of my life with her."

His brother gave him a low whistle. "That serious, huh?"

"As a heart attack. I even bought her a ring."

"Wow." The line fell silent for a few seconds. "Does Mom know about this?"

"No way. She hated Kourtney."

"And knowing that, you're still determined to marry her?"

"Mom just needs to see her for who she truly is." The Taurus in front of him turned down a side road, and Caleb floored the accelerator. "I've got to go, Adam. I'll let you know how it turns out."

****

Alex Leadbetter's heart jumped when she heard a car approach her mother's house. A 450-horsepower, seven-liter V8 semi-hemi that purred like a kitten when idle and roared like a lion when fully revved up. The perfect engine for a classic muscle car like a 1970 Phase III-SS 454 Camaro. And she knew only one person who drove a car like that.

Caleb Kelly.

She excused herself from the tedious conversation revolving around the seating at Kourtney's wedding reception and went to the front door. A peek out the window confirmed what she already knew, and her gut tightened. At the very far end of the driveway sat the midnight blue Camaro with white striping, and its owner was stomping up the walkway like a man on a mission.

Shit!

She should've known he'd come chasing after her older sister. Every idiot of a man did. She just hoped Caleb would've been different.

Or that he would've at least gotten the hint from the last few emails she'd sent him while posing as her sister. She'd purposely tried to prepare him for an empty apartment by hinting that "Kourtney" was getting bored in Ft. Walton and wanted to leave.

She slipped out the front door to intercept him before he banged on the door and blew a gasket in front of Kourtney and her sister's future in-laws. "Caleb," she said, pouring every ounce of Southern sweetness into her drawl, "what brings you here?"

He yanked off his aviator sunglasses, his blue eyes dark with fury, but her pulse fluttered like a giddy teenager's in front of her crush. Sweet Jesus, even while scowling, he made her head fuzzy. He was tall and lean, but his biceps bulged underneath his fitted T-shirt. His brown hair pushed at the limits of regulation length, the ends curling ever so slightly in the late April humidity. The man was walking, breathing temptation on two legs, and her self-absorbed sister definitely didn't deserve him.

"Where is she?"

So much for pleasantries. "Where's who?"

"Cut the crap, Alex. I know she's in there."

He tried to get past her, but she wedged her arms between the columns on the front porch of her mother's plantation-style home and blocked him. "What makes you think that?"

He pointed to the red BMW 335i in the driveway. "I know her car. Now let me in." He pried her arms down, sending a little shock through her that stunned her enough to let him by.

Then she regained her senses. She ran and plastered herself against the front door to keep him from barging inside. Part of her wanted him to go in and learn the truth about her sister. The other part wanted to spare him the pain. "Caleb, you really don't want to go in there."

"Why not?" He crossed his arms and continued to

scowl at her.

Time to see how much he knew. "Have you been following Kourtney on Facebook?"

"No, I wasn't allowed access to it while I was deployed." His jaw tightened, and a look of panic crossed his face. "What are you hiding from me? She's not pregnant or something, is she?"

If she were, you certainly wouldn't be the baby daddy. Her sister had moved back to Jackson Grove within a week of Caleb's departure to Afghanistan and immediately hooked up with Ryan McClure, heir to the McClure family timber fortune. Within three months, she'd gotten him to propose and started planning the biggest wedding this county had seen in over a decade. "No, she's not pregnant."

As far as I know. It would be like her sister to get knocked up just so she'd have some leverage over her fiancé.

"Then why won't you let me inside, Alex?"

She took a deep breath and offered a silent prayer, hoping he'd leave as soon as he learned the truth. "Because Kourtney's in there with her future in-laws finalizing the details for her wedding next weekend."

Caleb stumbled back like a man who'd just been punched in the gut. "She's getting married?"

His face paled, and when she touched his cheek, it was cool and clammy, despite the eighty-degree heat. "I'm sorry you had to find out this way—"

He silenced her by pushing her hand away and bolting for the door. "Kourtney?" he called into the house.

"Damn it, Caleb!" Alex spun around and chased after

him, running into his back when stopped suddenly at the entrance to the front parlor.

Now it was Kourtney's turn to go pale. Or at least as pale as she could go under the layers of orange-glow spray tan. Her brown eyes widened, and she rose unsteadily to her feet like she'd just seen a ghost. "Caleb, what are you doing here?"

"I could ask you the same thing." He glared at Ryan and curled his hands into fists. "I thought you were going to wait for me to come back from Afghanistan."

Kourtney swallowed, and her cool queen bee exterior fell back into place. "Didn't you get my note?"

"Yes."

"Then you know why I left," she said as though it was all his fault.

Ryan stood and wrapped his arm possessively around Kourtney's waist, his eyes narrowing in challenge as he stared at Caleb. "Besides, she's moved on to better things."

Caleb's fists flexed, and Alex's heart did a double-time skip. If this situation didn't get diffused soon, the groom would be sporting a black eye for the wedding, and Caleb would be spending more than one night in jail, especially since Ryan's father played golf with Judge Ramsey.

She moved between them and pushed Caleb back into the hallway. "Please don't make a scene," she whispered.

"I'm not leaving until I have answers."

"But this is not the proper time nor place."

"I need to talk to her."

"And you will, but let me try to smooth things over first."

Behind them, Ryan's father grumbled something about calling the police, and she pressed all her weight against Caleb's chest, shoving him a few inches closer to the door. "Do you remember the Iron Line bar in town?" she asked.

His attention finally flickered from Kourtney and Ryan to her. "Yes."

"Head over there and have a beer. Tell Earl to put it on my tab. I'll meet you as soon as I can get away from this mess."

He glanced over her shoulder at the crowd of people gathering around her overly distressed sister. Then he leveled those piercing blue eyes on her and said, "Fine, but if you're not there in an hour, I'll be back."

The look on his face showed he wouldn't leave so easily next time.

Alex exhaled a sigh of relief. With any luck, she wouldn't have to call J.T. to keep Caleb out of jail. "I'll be there faster than a swarm of ants on a picnic."

He took a few more steps back, his normally luscious mouth pressed in an unrelenting line, before turning around and letting himself out the front door. The Camaro roared to life like an angry jaguar, followed by the squeal of tires.

Don't you dare get pulled over being an ass. She might be best friends with the police chief's son, but friendship wouldn't protect Caleb from stupidity.

Alex turned around just as her mother strutted in from the front parlor. Her uptight walk could've been blamed on the fitted pencil skirt that clung to the former beauty queen's still-shapely legs, but the pursed-lip frown warned Alex it was time for her to leave, too.

"What was he doing here?" her mother demanded in an angry whisper.

"No idea." Alex tried to brush past her mother, but the pissed-off matriarch grabbed her by the arm and hauled her back.

"Don't give me any sass, Alexandra. What did he say to you?"

Alex rolled her eyes. "Just what you'd expect him to say after coming home and finding Kourtney gone. He was here for answers."

"He embarrassed us in front of the McClures."

"If Kourtney had handled breaking up with him like a grown-up, this wouldn't have happened."

"Why didn't you try to stop him? Do you have any idea how much he upset your sister?" Her mother donned the same wounded Southern belle simper Kourtney had worn minutes before.

Alex massaged her temples. She had to get out of this crazy house before she said something she regretted. Or worse, before Caleb came charging back in. "Let me handle him, Mama. You go back to the McClures, and I'll make sure he doesn't make another scene."

She grabbed her keys off the hook by the front door and ran to her rebuilt '57 Chevy pickup. When her engine started, it was a low, barrel-chested growl. Solid and reassuring, not predatory. But she liked it that way.

Sweat coated her palms as she drove into town. She needed to know the real reason Caleb was in town, and prayed to God it wasn't because of her emails.

CHAPTER TWO

Caleb pulled the label from his bottle of Bud and soaked in the atmosphere of the nearly empty bar. The last time he'd been here, it was right in the middle of football season, and the place had been packed. A wide gray line painted along the walls and floor divided the interior into two sides, each with their own entrance. The Alabama side was decorated in crimson and white; the Auburn side, orange and blue. And from what he remembered, most of the locals didn't cross the iron gray line once they picked a side. He'd chosen one of the few tables in the neutral territory since he couldn't remember which side Alex preferred.

His mind drifted back to the scene at the house, and his head swam. Kourtney hadn't just left him—she was marrying someone else. How long had that been going on? Had she been secretly seeing that guy while sending him those emails? And if so, should he believe anything she said?

Do I even know her at all?

His stomach churned at the question. Worse, he'd left before he'd gotten the answers he'd driven hours to get.

"Hey, Earl, how are the Braves doing?" a familiar voice asked as the door swung open on the orange and blue side. Alex strode into the building like she owned it.

"We're up by a run," the older man behind the counter replied and pointed to Caleb. "Your friend's over there."

"Awesome. Do you mind if I help myself?" She jumped up onto the bar without waiting for an answer and swung her legs over in a blur of skirts and cowboy boots. She reached into the fridge and pulled out four bottles of beer. "Just put these on my tab."

"How about you just apply those to the cost of that new battery I need installed?"

"I like the way you think." She grinned, her nose and eyes crinkling, and popped the top off one of the bottles before putting the other three in a bucket of ice.

As she cracked another joke with Earl, Caleb studied Alex. She was as different from her older sister as two siblings could be. She lacked Kourtney's curves and elegant blond refinement. Alex's auburn hair tumbled past her shoulders in messy waves, and he wondered how much pressure she'd been put under to wear the sleeveless dress that clung to her lean figure before flaring out around her hips. A few freckles lay splattered across her nose and cheeks, but they only enhanced her girl-next-door image. Even though he'd been dating her sister, he'd always found Alex easy to talk to, especially since she shared his love for classic cars.

But as she made her way to him, her steps slowed, and her grin turned hollow. She set the bucket on the table and slumped into the chair across from him. "I see you decided to play it safe here," she said, first pointing to the gray line beneath the table and then at his half-drunk bottle of Bud.

"I'm only here for answers."

"I was afraid of that." She took a long swig of her beer. "So, what do you want to know?"

"How long has Kourtney been back?"

Alex's brown eyes widened, and she took another long drink. "A while."

"How long?"

She finished off the remaining beer in the bottle and reached for a new one. "Listen, I know what my sister did to you was really shitty—"

"How long?" he repeated, this time with a growl edging into his voice. The more she evaded his question, the tighter his gut squeezed.

Alex focused her gaze on the bottle in her hand as she opened it. "She moved back home shortly after you left."

He jumped to his feet, his hands curling into fists. He needed to punch something now. "Motherf—"

"Hey, watch your language." She rose from her chair and pushed him back into his, handing him her open bottle in the process. "Here, drink this and calm down before I have to call in a favor to keep you out of jail."

Now it was his turn to take a long swig. The beer she'd given him was more intense than the bland lager he'd been drinking, with a strange fruity note at the end. He glanced at the label. "Purple Haze?"

"Yeah, I know—girly beer. But at least it goes down easily." As though to prove her point, she opened another bottle for herself and took another long drink. "So, tell me the real reason why you're here."

The anger drained from his shoulders, and he slid back in his chair. It had been bad enough to come home and

12

find the woman he'd come to love gone, but now he was reeling from the shock that she'd moved on so quickly. "You wouldn't understand."

"Try me." She gave him that relaxed smile that reminded him how easy she was to talk to.

"What's the use? She's marrying that prick in a week."

Alex snorted with a laugh. "You're dead-on about Ryan. And technically, it's less than a week since the wedding is Saturday."

Caleb groaned and pressed his palms to his face, dragging the heels of his hand from his eyes to his temples. "This is not the homecoming I was expecting."

"What were you expecting?" she asked, her voice unusually serious.

"Kourtney, waiting for me at the airfield with the other families, ready to welcome me back by wrapping her arms around me and giving me a kiss that would help me forget about all the shit I'd gone through during the last nine months."

Alex nodded, her gaze sympathetic. "I'm sorry she did this to you."

"Not as sorry as I am. I knew she didn't like the idea of me being gone for so long, but I figured she'd at least wait for me to come home, especially since each letter she'd sent me seemed to imply that."

"Shit," Alex whispered under her breath before gulping her beer. "Would it help if I told you you'd be better off without her?"

He snorted. "I know you don't get along well with your sister—"

"That's putting it mildly."

13

"But you don't know her like I do."

Another snort, this time without the mirth. "That's where you're wrong. I know her far better than you ever will, and as much as I hate to say it, I'm not surprised she did what she did."

He stiffened like she'd just drenched him with cold water. "Why?"

"Because Kourtney has always needed to be the center of attention. Your deployment left her alone with no one to worship her, so she came back here and found a new dumbass who was wowed enough by her cleavage to tolerate her behavior."

It would be all too easy to accept Alex's explanation and walk away, but he couldn't forget the woman who'd written those emails.

Courage is doing what you know is right, even when you're afraid. Hope is what gets us through the dark moments when we doubt ourselves. And love is what makes the impossible possible.

He closed his eyes and let her words ease the doubt in his soul. That was the Kourtney he wanted to know. She was more than just a pretty face. She also had a beautiful heart that spoke to him in a way no other woman had.

"I just want a chance to talk to her."

"Why?"

"Because I know if I get her alone and let her know how much she means to me, she'd come back."

"She really has you wrapped around her little finger, doesn't she?"

"Maybe," he said with a half smile and ran his hand over the good luck charm in his pocket. "Do you think you can help me win her back?"

Alex choked on her beer. "Me?"

"Yeah. After all, you said you know her better than anyone else."

"I think you need your head examined."

"Come on, Alex. Who would you rather have as a brother-in-law? Me or that prick?"

She banged her empty bottle on the table. "Holy crap! You weren't thinking of marrying her, were you?"

"Should I show you the ring I bought her?"

"No, no, no, no!" Alex massaged her fingertips into her forehead. "Why are guys so fucking stupid?"

"And you were the one telling me to watch my language." He took a sip of the raspberry-flavored beer, his mood lightening. He was wearing her down, and if he could get Alex on board, she'd help him find a way to get Kourtney back. "So, would you be willing to be my wingman?"

"Give me one good reason why you're so head-over-heels stupid for my Barbie-doll sister." She reached for the last bottle in the bucket.

"Are you going to be okay to drive?"

"I live two blocks down the road. I walked over here." She opened the bottle, catching the edge of the top against the table and smacking it firmly with her hand. She draped her arm across the back of her chair and crossed her boot-clad legs, doubt written all over face. "If you want my help, you need to convince me that you love Kourtney for more than just her double-Ds."

He raked his fingers through his hair, unsure how much he should reveal from those deeply personal letters. "Can't you just take my word for it?"

"Nope." She grinned before raising the fresh bottle to her lips.

"Fine, you win." He took a drink to steel his courage before spilling his guts. "Afghanistan wasn't a fun place to be, especially in the middle of a war."

"No shit. My friend J.T. still has nightmares about that place."

"Then you have some idea how it was over there. I saw things I never want to see again. But no matter how dark it got, your sister always had something to say to bring me back into the light. Whenever I felt like there was nothing good left in this world, I'd always find an email from her that reminded me that things weren't as bleak as I imagined them to be. That's why I fell in love with her."

Alex's face blanched, making her freckles stand out more than before. She finished off her bottle like a college student trying to set a funneling speed record and squeezed her eyes shut afterward. Her face tightened in pain, drawing her shoulders up toward her ears. A full minute ticked by before she finally said, "Damn it. I wish you hadn't said that."

"Now you know why I want her back."

When Alex opened her eyes, a mixture of grief and pity shimmered from their brown depths. "But what if she doesn't want you anymore?"

Caleb swallowed hard. It wasn't something he was ready to consider. Not yet. "All I need is a chance to speak with her alone, to find out what changed while I was gone."

Alex stared at the floor and chewed her bottom lip, the empty bottle in her hands rocking from side to side. "I think I'm going to need another drink."

He eyed the collection of empty bottles on the table. "I think you've had enough, Alex."

She shook her head. "If you've had the day I've had, you'd need a six pack, too."

But she set the bottle on the table and smoothed her dress over her lap. "So, all you want is a chance to talk to Kourtney alone?"

"Are you agreeing to help me?"

She finally met his gaze, her eyes sharp and clever as though she hadn't had a single drop of beer. "Maybe."

"Maybe?" he asked, arching a brow.

"I'll need a favor from you in exchange, as well as your complete cooperation with my plan."

He crossed his arms and leaned back. "What are your terms?"

A mischievous smile curled her lips. "First off, if I'm going to be your wingman, you will never, ever, refer to me as 'Goose.'"

For the first time since he'd left home, a full-bodied laugh erupted from his chest. "Agreed. We'll have to come up with a unique call sign for you."

"Second, how long can you stay in town? If my plan is going to work, we'll need a few days."

This sounded promising. "I can stay until Sunday morning. Even though I'm on my post-deployment R&R, I have to report back to Eglin so I can meet the movers Monday morning."

"Plenty of time. Where are you staying?"

Uh-oh—the first hiccup in his hastily thrown together plan just revealed itself. He'd been so certain he'd be able to coax Kourtney back that he hadn't even thought about overnight accommodations. Hell, he hadn't even packed a suitcase.

And Alex knew it, judging by the "I thought so" expression on her face. "Let me make a phone call."

She pulled out her cell and punched in a number. "Hello, Miss Martha, how are you this evening?" After a few uh-huhs and a "You're so sweet," she continued. "Do you have any rooms available at your B&B? My date for the wedding just got into town, and he needs a place to stay."

Her date for the wedding? A moment of panic kicked his heart into high gear, but Alex just kept on going as though nothing was wrong with this scenario.

"Well, I would invite him to stay with me—once you get a look at him, you'll understand why—but I don't want to set tongues wagging."

Oh, she'd definitely have one wagging tongue—his. Not to mention her sister's.

"You only have a room available until Wednesday morning, huh?" She slid her gaze back to him, her drawl becoming more syrupy by the second as she twirled her hair around her finger. "That should be fine. Perhaps by then, I won't care about my reputation."

He could almost hear the other woman on the line giggling with Alex.

"That's so sweet of you. I'll send him over in a bit. Thank you again." She ended the call and set her phone on the table. "I've got you a room at the Honey Bee Bed and Breakfast for the next three nights. Miss Martha's a great cook, so you're in for a treat."

"Back up a minute, Alex. What's this about me being your date for the wedding?"

"That's where my plan comes into action. Mama and Kourtney have been harping on me for weeks because I don't have a date for the wedding, so if you pose as my date, that gets them off my back for a few seconds."

"Just one problem—I'm here to convince your sister to marry me, not sit beside you as she marries that asshole."

She reached for his half-drunk bottle of Purple Haze and helped herself to a drink from it. "Just hear me out. As my date for the wedding, you're automatically invited to all the pre-wedding bullshit, meaning you'll have more access to my sister."

His jaw fell lax. He hadn't considered that.

"Furthermore, I know my sister, remember? I know for a fact she always wants what she can't have. If she sees the two of us together, she'll want you even more, especially if she thinks you've moved on to me of all people."

"Are you sure of that?"

"Do I look like I'm trying to pull a fast one on you?"

No, Alex had never been one to beat around the bush. She was frank and direct, more one of the guys than some girl who got off on playing head games with men. And as crazy as her plan sounded, it might actually work. "What's the rest of your plan?"

She dragged her chair to his side of the table and beckoned for him to lean in closer as she dropped her voice. "Starting tonight, we'll show up in places where I know the town gossips will be and act like we can't keep our hands off of each other. It'll get back to Kourtney, and when we show up at Mama's house on Wednesday afternoon to help with the reception favors, Kourtney will be so crazy with jealousy that you'll have her in the palm of your hand."

It almost seemed too easy, except for one small problem. He'd have to pretend to be crazy about Alex when all he could think about was her sister. "And you're okay with me using you like this?"

He didn't miss the flicker of pain in her eyes or the way her smile tightened. "It's not like guys haven't done it before. I'm used to them pretending to like me only to get closer to Kourtney."

That was the only hitch in her otherwise perfect plan. Alex was a nice girl, one he'd consider introducing to his brothers. She was fun, no-nonsense, always grinning. Hell, if he hadn't met Kourtney first, he might have considered dating her. "Listen, Alex, I don't want to hurt you—"

"Who said anything about me getting hurt? This is my idea, after all. And I know going into it that you have your heart set on my sister, so there's no deception or anything on your part. Just do me one favor, though."

"What's that?"

"Just don't call me by her name."

He forced a chuckle to bust up the awkwardness of her request. "I doubt we'll find ourselves in a situation where I'd mistake you for her."

"Maybe not, but I'm finally feeling those beers kicking in so I won't be responsible for my behavior in about fifteen minutes."

"Then perhaps we should get your plan in motion before you pass out and I have to carry you home."

She giggled. "That definitely would set the town

talking."

The door to the crimson and white side of the bar opened, and a couple strolled in. He recognized the woman as one of Kourtney's friends, but he couldn't remember her name. And judging by the narrow-eyed look of suspicion that she gave him and Alex, she probably recognized him, too.

Alex grabbed his T-shirt and pulled his attention back to her. "Kiss me," she whispered.

"What?"

She answered him by pressing her lips to his. He stiffened from the initial shock of it, his mind still reeling that another woman was kissing him. Then the next shock hit him—he was enjoying it. Alex ran her tongue along the seam of his mouth, begging for entry to his mouth, and like a stunned fool, he gave it to her.

Kourtney's kiss had been sharp and electric, a bolt of lightning that surged through him and in a matter of seconds left him harder than a horny teenager. Alex's kiss was more like a fire on a cold day or a cup of morning coffee. It spread through his veins with the same easygoing nature she embodied. He followed her lead, his tongue twirling around hers until he almost forgot why he was in this small town in the first place. His mind screamed at him to stop, but his body refused to listen. He longed for the warmth and comfort her kiss offered, for the sense of coming home he'd desired when he stepped off the plane. He wrapped his arms around her waist and drew her closer until she was practically sitting in his lap, eager to enjoy everything she so willingly offered.

And that was when she pulled away. Her bottom lip

trembled, and her breaths came fast and deep. "Not bad, flyboy."

Oh, shit, what have I done?

Alex clamped her hands around his cheeks and held his gaze on her. "Don't think about it, Caleb. Remember our plan."

Easy for her to say. She isn't the one getting caught in a compromising position.

"Just look at me and listen," she continued in a low, calm voice. "The woman who just walked in—what is she doing?"

He glanced over her shoulder at the couple. "She's pulling out her phone and texting."

"Good. Now, we're going to leave here hand in hand and go to your car. Understand?"

He nodded, offering a silent prayer he hadn't royally fucked things up by agreeing to Alex's plan.

"Arm around my waist," she murmured. "Remember, we want everyone to think you're all into me."

He continued the ruse until they were safely shielded by his car. Then, he released her and leaned on the hood of his Camaro, staring at his reflection and wondering when everything went to hell. "That wasn't what I was expecting."

Alex leaned against the car next to him and crossed her arms, not displaying an ounce of his worry. "Really? I thought it went quite well."

"What are you talking about? I was groping you in front of one of Kourtney's friends."

"Just as I'd expected you to do. Lynette's probably telling my sister all about the very believable performance you just gave." She tilted his chin up. "Relax, Caleb. Everything is going according to plan."

He wished he could share her confidence. Instead, all he felt was disgust at his behavior. It was one thing to fake a kiss. It was an entirely different matter to lose himself in it, especially when his heart belonged to another woman. "I feel like I'm cheating on her."

"Bullshit. Besides, it's not like she wasn't cheating on you while you were gone."

"Way to twist the knife in my gut. While you're at it, care to slide a few hundred splinters into my skin and set them on fire?"

"Ooh, I never suspected you were the kinky type." She took his hands and turned him around so he was sitting on the edge of the hood. "Listen, Caleb, don't beat yourself up. Remember, I'm in on this, too, and I know the only reason why you even pretended to enjoy kissing me was because of our agreement to help you get my sister back."

That was the problem—he hadn't been pretending.

"I know I'm Kourtney's hideous little sister—"

"You're not hideous."

"I'm not her."

"No," he agreed. Kourtney screamed sex, from her pale blond hair to the generous cleavage and hourglass curves that made him the envy of every man in his unit. Alex was tall and slender, her boyish figure complimenting her tomboyish disposition. "But you're cute."

She groaned. "Now it's my turn to have a knife twist in my gut. Calling a girl cute is the equivalent of telling her she has a nice personality."

"You do have a nice personality."

"Stop it!" she teased, her laughter infecting him and driving away his guilt. "And I suppose you'd love to introduce me to one of your friends, but they're already all in relationships, right?"

"Actually, I was thinking one of my brothers…"

"Enough!" She released his hands and wrapped her arms around his neck. "A girl can only take so much."

Before he realized what he was doing, his hands were back around her waist, and they were leaning against his car like a happy couple. It surprised him how easily it happened, as though they'd been out on a real date rather than setting a plan in motion to deceive everyone around them.

"So you're not mad at me for jumping the gun and kissing you in front of Lynette?"

"No, I'm not." He stared at her, wondering why he hadn't noticed how well her thick lashes framed her warm brown eyes before. "And I was wrong about the cute thing—you're actually kind of pretty."

"Keep it up, flyboy, and you may be battling your baby brother for the best acting performance of the year." A wave of color rose into her cheeks, and her attention shifted to the Camaro. "You know, I'm seriously in love with your car."

"Is that so?"

She nodded. "You wouldn't believe the fantasies I have about it."

"Now who's the kinky one?" He'd intended just to give her a friendly jostle, but it ended up pressing her body against his and awakening a whole new level of awareness. She fit well in his arms. Almost too well.

Her breath caught, and she stilled against him. Her fingers grazed the nape of his neck, setting off a flurry of erotic explosions from the seemingly innocent touch. That little voice of warning begged him to let go, but he needed to find out if that kiss in the bar was nothing more than a fluke.

This time, he initiated the kiss and controlled it. No tongue. No open-mouth devouring of the other person. But it didn't matter. Just the pressure of her lips evoked the same reaction as before.

Correction—the reaction was even stronger than before. He ran his hands up her back, pulling her even closer until they were connected from their lips to their thighs. This was what he'd imagined it would be like when he got home and kissed Kourtney after all those months apart. This was what he dreamt about when he closed his eyes in the barracks every night.

But when he opened his eyes, he caught a glimpse of Alex's wild red hair and froze.

She pulled away, her face downcast, but didn't remove her arms from his neck.

"I'm sorry, Alex."

"Don't apologize."

"I don't know what came over me."

"Don't worry about it."

But the hurt in her voice did worry him. "If you think this is a bad idea—"

"I'm fine." She lifted her face, revealing a new mask of indifference he'd never expected from her. "But I think we've done enough for tonight."

"Agreed." If he spent any more time fertilizing this

25

fake romance, he might end up in deep shit. "So, what's the next step in your plan?"

"You're going to get some rest at Miss Martha's. Just turn right at the gas station, go two blocks, and make a left. It's the big yellow Victorian house."

He mentally repeated her instructions and nodded. "And then?"

She peeked over his shoulder into his car. "I don't see a suitcase in there."

"I didn't have time to pack."

"I figured as much." She let go of him and stepped back. "There's a Wal-Mart on the edge of town that way. Or, if you're too hoity-toity to shop there, then you're looking at a half-hour's drive to Opelika for clothes."

"I'll go shopping tomorrow." Today already had him more confused than he cared to admit.

"Good. Then meet me at the shop tomorrow around 5:30. We'll go from there."

"Sounds good." Maybe by then he'd be able to control his body better.

Or at least figure out why he forgot all about Kourtney when he was kissing her sister.

"All righty, then." She took another step back, looking more like an awkward teenager who'd just spoken to her high school crush. "Just be careful around Miss Martha— she's been known to let men know how much she appreciates their backsides with a little pinch."

"Now you tell me." The tension vanished, and they were back to the way they had always been, teasing each other good-naturedly and sharing a laugh. "If my ass is bruised in the morning, I'm blaming you."

"It's not my fault you have a cute ass."

He climbed into the driver's seat with a grin, but as he drove off, it faded.

What the hell had just happened?

And worse, what had he gotten himself into?

CHAPTER THREE

Alex straightened up from under the hood of a late-model Lincoln Town Car and wiped the grease off her hands with a shop cloth. God, she hated messes like this, especially when they could've been prevented in the first place. "How many miles do you have on this, Miss Martha?"

"Oh, I don't know," the older woman replied, her eyes rolling left and then up toward the ceiling. "Maybe a hundred and twenty thousand miles."

Jermaine, one of the other mechanics, checked the odometer and shook his head. "I think you're confusing that seven for a two, Miss Martha."

"Oh?" she asked innocently.

Alex silently cursed. "It looks like your timing belt went out. You were supposed to have changed it at around a hundred and fifty thousand miles."

"How long will it take you to replace it?

Now came the hard part—delivering the bad news. "If I had gotten to it before it snapped, it would've been just a few hours of labor. But now that it's gone, I need to check your cylinders and make sure none of them were damaged. And if some of them were, then we need to discuss whether or not you want me to rebuild the engine or just scrap the car."

The older lady tightened her purse to her chest.

Please don't have a heart attack on me.

"Oh, dear," Miss Martha said in a higher voice than normal, "how much would that cost?"

"Two to three thousand, depending on how much damage there is."

"Oh, dear." She started to sink, but Jermaine steadied her long enough to guide her back to the chair against the wall. "I don't have that kind of money on hand."

Not many people did unless they were the McClures or the Ramseys or one of the other big families in town. Most of the people in Jackson Grove were blue-collar folks who worked in the lumber or paper mills around town. That was the only downside to having the only car shop in area—she was a cause for some of the major expenses they were dealt.

Alex gave her hands one final wipe and tossed the towel into the laundry bin. "Come into my office, and let's talk some more about this in an air-conditioned room."

She closed the door behind them and waited for the older lady to sit down before speaking. "I'm sorry to be the bearer of bad news."

"No, it's okay, Alex. I knew the car was getting old, but Hank always took care of these things for me, and after he passed, I just forgot about tune-ups and the like." Miss Martha's eyes teared up at the mention of her late husband, and Alex reached for the box of tissues on her desk.

"I understand if you don't want me to work on the car."

29

"No, I need a working car, and I definitely can't afford a new one."

Alex peeked out the window to make sure no one was nearby to overhear what she was about to suggest. "I tell you what—let's make a little deal. You were kind enough to give Caleb a room on short notice, so why don't we just do a trade. I'll fix your car in exchange for you letting him stay at your B&B those three nights."

"But Alex, dear, that doesn't equal the cost of the repair."

"I know it doesn't, but in a town this small, we all need to look out for each other."

"No, I simply can't agree to this. I feel like I'd be taking advantage of you."

Damn Southern pride. Alex looked out into her garage and came up with a new game plan. "You know, Miss Martha, you're probably one of the best cooks in town."

"Why, thank you, dear."

"And I know my boys would appreciate a nice breakfast or lunch from time to time. How about you throw in a few catered meals for us so we can call it even?"

The older woman's foggy blue eyes brightened, and a smile returned to her face. "Now that sounds like something I can agree to."

"Sounds like a plan. Let me do a little more digging in your engine, and once I get the final estimate, we can negotiate how many meals that would be."

"Bless you, child. I don't know what I'd do without you. You have your father's heart—always looking out for everyone in town."

Alex forced the smile to stay in place when Miss Martha mentioned her father. He'd been born and raised in this town, and after law school, he'd come back here to practice. Over the years, he'd taken more and more responsibility for the community onto his shoulders, from writing out wills to helping the local unions negotiate contracts with the mills to serving as mayor. In the end, the stress was his undoing, triggering the heart attack that had ended his life way too soon.

He was also the one who fostered her love of cars, and every time she stepped foot in the shop, she thought about him.

She noticed the minute hand on the clock sweep over the six. It was quitting time. "I'll give you a call tomorrow with the estimate."

"Thank you again, Alex."

"No problem, but please, let's keep this between the two of us."

"Of course, dear." The older woman paused at the door, a mass of wrinkles gathering around her mouth and eyes as she grinned. "And you were right about that young man—he's definitely a looker. If I were about fifty years younger, I'd be all over him."

Alex wondered how many times she'd already "accidentally" brushed against Caleb's bottom since he'd arrived.

As if on cue, the man in question strolled into the shop, earning a flirtatious little wave from the B&B owner. "I'll see you in the morning, Caleb."

Alex fought back a laugh from the look of panic that flashed across his face. He gave Miss Martha wide berth as she left the shop.

"How's your ass?" she teased.

"Don't ask." He pointed to a large splatter of oil under the oval nametag on her coveralls. "Cute."

"Hey, I'm a working girl." She'd given up years ago on trying to be as neat and pretty as her sister. She was much more comfortable with grease on her hands than makeup on her face. "Sorry for the mess. Just give me a few minutes to get cleaned up, and we can go get dinner."

"Just a few minutes?"

"Yes, just a few minutes. Unlike Kourtney, I don't require an hour of prep work to go out. Besides, I think you'll enjoy seeing this." She poked her head into the main garage. "Jermaine, I'm done for the day. Can you lock up?"

"Sure thing, Alex."

As she led Caleb up the stairs to her apartment above the shop, she heard the familiar clang of the metal garage doors closing. By the time they were ready to leave, her crew would have the shop tucked in for the night. Alex unlocked the door to the second floor of the converted warehouse and motioned for him to follow her to her private workspace that was separate from the rest of her living quarters. "Take a look at this baby," she said she opened the door.

Caleb's mouth fell open. "Is that a Roadrunner?"

She nodded, her chest swelling with pride. "Yep, a 1971 Plymouth Roadrunner with a retractable air grabber and a 440 six pack."

"Nice." He ran his hand along the freshly painted hood with its orange and black stripes. "How did you get it up here?"

"This used to be a cotton warehouse, and it's sitting on a lift that goes down into the garage." She pointed out the metal arms that were folded neatly along the floor around the car. "When I'm done, I'll be able to drop it down into the garage and give it a whirl."

"How much work's left on it?"

"I'm still putting the engine back together, and I'm waiting for another bucket seat to come in from the upholsterer, but I'm getting close to finishing it."

"Sweet."

"Take your time checking it out while I get a quick shower."

"I definitely will," he replied, his eyes never leaving the car.

That was one thing she always liked about Caleb. He got her obsession with the classic muscle cars of the sixties and seventies. Not many people did, especially not her mom and her sister. Her dad had, though.

Alex ducked into the shower long enough to scrub all the grime off her skin and put on a simple T-shirt with her favorite pair of denim cutoffs and sandals. Her damp hair fell over her shoulders in a tousled mess. She'd given up on straightening it years ago. As soon as she stepped outside in the humidity, it would curl up again.

She found Caleb where she'd left him, still fawning over the rebuilt Roadrunner. "Where did you get this stereo console?"

"I found a guy online who makes face plates that look like the originals so I could have my HD radio without detracting too much from the ambience."

"I like it." He climbed out of the driver's seat and ran his hands lovingly over the top of the car. "You've done a fine job on this."

"Thanks. I wish I could say it was a restoration, but it needed some updates, especially if I wanted to make that engine a little more fuel efficient."

"These cars are all about horsepower, Alex, not miles per gallon." He gave the car one final pat before turning his attention to her. "So, what's the game plan for tonight?"

"We're having dinner at the Sugar Belle Café."

"Any reason why?"

She grinned, but that didn't stop the butterflies that were multiplying in her stomach. Time to put her plan into action. She hadn't been lying when she told Caleb that it would drive her sister nuts to hear he'd moved on to someone else. She only hoped that by the time Kourtney tried to woo him back, he'd already be head over heels for her. After all, she was the one who'd written those letters. Now she needed him to see she was the girl he wanted, not Kourtney. "Do you know who meets there every Monday night for pie and gossip?"

He dug his hands into the back pockets of his jeans. "I'm scared to ask."

"The Junior League." She took his hand and pulled him toward the door. "Normally, Mama and Kourtney would be there, as they are members of the organization, but with the wedding so close, they'll regretfully be absent. However, all of their friends will be there."

"And you think a repeat of last night will spark Kourtney's jealousy?"

"No guarantee, but it will definitely get back to her. Of course, Miss Ada runs a respectable establishment, so we may need to tone it down a notch."

Caleb ran his hand through his freshly buzzed hair and hesitated at the top of the stairs. "It just seems wrong, like I'm cheating on her."

The butterflies hardened into a lump of stone and sank in the pit of her belly. *Please don't let him back out before I have a chance to convince him that I'm the one he wants.*

She gulped back her fear and scrambled for an answer. "You're not cheating on her. After all, she's the one who dumped you and hopped into the next man's bed."

He pressed his lips together. "Gee, thanks for making me feel better."

"Just stating the facts. Besides, we've only exchanged a few fake kisses. It's not like we're sleeping together." Although she wouldn't turn him down if he offered, provided that it wasn't just rebound sex.

On the other hand, rebound sex with Caleb Kelly may be worth the damage it would do to her heart.

"Yeah, they were just fake kisses," he repeated as though he were trying to convince himself of that.

Her pulse shifted into high gear. Maybe he'd enjoyed those kisses as much as she had. Score one point in her favor. "I promise to keep my lips off yours tonight, if you want."

Of course, she made no promises about her hands.

"Let's just play it by ear." He traipsed down the stairs to the back door of the garage. "So, it's just dinner tonight? No public make-out session?"

She giggled. "Nope, not tonight. And tomorrow is an

even more private event."

"Sounds like you have the whole week planned out."

"This is entirely my idea, and I'll take full responsibility for it. Tonight, we just need to act like a cute couple in front of the gossipmongers. Tomorrow, we're going on an outing with a couple of my friends, and by Wednesday, I bet you my 440 six pack that Kourtney will jealous enough to single you out when we go over to Mama's to help with the wedding favors."

"And then I'll have my time alone with her to find out what the hell happened."

"Bingo. Now, put your game face on. We're heading into battle." She looped her arm through his and led him across the street to the Sugar Belle Café.

They walked through the front door to the mostly empty restaurant, but that didn't stop her from draping herself over him when the owner approached them from behind the lunch counter. "Evening, Alex," she said, her white teeth sparkling against her dark skin in a welcoming smile. "What brings you in tonight? I thought you'd be at your mama's helping out with the wedding."

"They don't need me until later this week. Besides, I wanted to bring Caleb in for some of your sinfully delicious cooking."

"I'll be more than happy to give him some. The boy could use a good meal or two. Take a seat anywhere except for that big table, and I'll be over with some menus."

"And some sweet tea." Alex scanned the restaurant and chose a booth in clear view of the Junior League table. She slid in and pulled Caleb into the seat next to her. "When the ladies come in, you know what to do," she whispered, nodding to the table set for twenty.

"When will they be arriving?"

"In about five to ten minutes." She fixed a smile on her face as Miss Ada arrived with the menus. "What's the special today?"

"Fried ham steak."

"With your famous greens?"

"You know it, darlin'."

Alex slid her menu to the end of the table without opening it. "Sold!"

Caleb, however, stared at the menu like it was written in another language. "I'm going to need a few minutes."

"Take your time. I'll be right over with those sweet teas." Miss Ada stepped behind the counter to fetch their drinks, giving Alex a few seconds alone with him.

"What's wrong?"

"I'm trying to figure out what I can eat here without paying for it later."

"Oh, I forgot—you're lactose intolerant, right?" She scooted next to him and peered at his menu. "I'd say go with the special."

He wrinkled his nose. "I'm not a huge fan of greens."

"You can get another side like fried okra or green beans, silly." She playfully batted him on the nose as the bell above the door announced the arrival of a new patron.

Mrs. Patty Jefferies, one of her mother's oldest friends, scanned the restaurant until her hard gaze settled on Alex.

Alex wrapped her arms around Caleb's neck and murmured in his ear, "Time for another Academy Award–winning performance."

"Yes, ma'am." He nuzzled her cheek, his breath warming her skin. "But you still haven't helped me decide what I want for dinner."

She was tempted to tell him to forget dinner and go straight to dessert, especially once his hand started inching up her bare thigh. Using the menu to shield them from prying eyes, she leaned into him. "I'm still voting for the ham and greens."

"And I'm telling you I don't like greens."

"I would recommend the country fried steak, but that has buttermilk gravy."

"Um-hmm."

Her breath caught as his other hand worked up the back of her shirt, tracing tiny circles along the base of her spine. Sweet Jesus, if he kept that up, she'd be hauling him back to her bed before dinner arrived. "It's kind of hard to think clearly when you're doing that, you know."

"Now you know how I felt when you ambushed me with that first kiss last night." He pulled back with a wicked grin that told her how much he enjoyed teasing her.

She whacked him with the menu. "Behave."

By then, three more of her mother's friends had join Mrs. Jefferies at the Junior League table, their heads all close together as they whispered at a frantic pace and glanced her way.

Alex resisted the urge to do a little victory dance. By tomorrow morning, the whole town would know about her and Caleb.

Miss Ada arrived with their teas. "Decide on anything?"

Caleb went to the menu, but Alex lowered it. "The

Yankee wants to play it safe with some fried chicken and green beans, Miss Ada."

"Hey now—" he protested, but she cut him off.

"I would love an extra side of fried okra, though, and of course, some of that yummy peach cobbler for dessert, please."

Miss Ada chuckled and took the menu. "I'll be out with your supper in a few."

"Yankee?" Caleb asked once they were alone again.

"Last I checked, Chicago was north of here."

"But do you have to act like the Civil War is still going on?"

"Shh!" She pressed her finger to his lips. "Some folks around here haven't gotten the memo that it's over."

Two more ladies came into the restaurant, both of them Kourtney's age, and immediately joined the chatter at the table.

Alex swung her legs onto Caleb's lap and pulled him closer. "In a few minutes, one of those ladies is going to pull out her phone and tattle on us."

"Then let's give them something to talk about." He made no effort to hide his hand on her thigh just before his lips covered hers.

Just like with last night's kisses, a series of fireworks exploded inside her from the first second of contact and sent her blood rushing into her cheeks. But as the kiss deepened into something slow and sensual, the heat spread to other parts of her body. Alex ran her fingers over the newly shaved short hair along the base of his scalp, the scratchy sensation contrasting with the firm massage of his hands on her thigh and sending delicious shivers through her.

Damn, he knew how to turn a woman on. Maybe it was time to remind him they were only faking this relationship.

Or maybe he wasn't into faking it anymore. She sure as hell wasn't.

A disgusted huff came from the Junior League table, and Alex forced herself to end the kiss. "I thought we were trying to avoid the public make-out session."

"Just following your lead."

"Bullshit."

"I like that you aren't afraid to call me on that." He turned her around so her legs fell off his lap and draped his arm around her shoulders. "And you were right about the phones."

Sure enough, both Mrs. Jefferies and her daughter, Mindy, were each talking in hushed tones to someone on their cells. And judging by the number of times they glanced her way during the conversation, Mama and Kourtney were getting an earful of her "disgraceful" behavior. "I know how this town works."

"And for that, I'm grateful."

Two plates of steaming food interrupted them. "Here you go," Miss Ada said as she set them down. "Now you show that boy what kind of good vittles he's missing out on."

"I sure will, Miss Ada." Alex dug her fork into the sweet and sour greens and stuffed her mouth with them.

"I'm still not brave enough to try those." He did, however, sample the green beans. After one nibble, he was devouring them. "I've always wondered one thing about you southerners. Why do you call the women here 'Miss' so-and-so?"

"Because we don't want to get smacked on the back of the head for being disrespectful. It's sort of how you always add 'ma'am' or 'sir' when you're speaking to a commanding officer."

"So if I start calling the owner of the B&B 'Miss Martha,' I won't get pinched?"

"Not likely. You have a fine ass, Captain Kelly, and Miss Martha must genuinely appreciate it." She grinned and added, "Maybe I should start letting you know how much I appreciate it, too."

He caught her hand a second before she struck. "Don't even think about it."

"Should I do something else to the cute ass of yours?"

His eyes darkened with desire, and her mouth went dry. He was finally starting to see her as a sexy woman in her own right, not just Kourtney's flat-chested little sister. "What are you suggesting?"

"Be a good boy and maybe you'll find out." She twisted her hand free and went back to her supper. "But first, you need to try Miss Ada's greens."

"Alex, I've already told you I don't—"

She silenced him with a forkful of the dark emerald wilted greens. Miss Ada sweetened them with plenty of brown sugar and bit of balsamic vinegar, which tempered the bitter sulfur taste most greens suffered from. The smoky hint of bacon balanced them out and added a richness that only pork grease could accomplish. The result was something purely divine, and it was time Caleb experienced them.

His eyes widened, but he didn't spit them out. Instead,

he chewed for a few seconds, swallowed, and immediately went for her plate. "Hey, those aren't half bad."

She yanked her plate out of reach. "I told you they were good." But after he made several more attempts to nab some from her plate, she conceded and let him have a few more bites.

"I can't believe Kourtney never took me here," he said after sampling the fried chicken and fried okra. "I never thought I'd enjoy Southern cooking so much."

"Kourtney thinks this place is beneath her. She only comes for the weekly meetings, and then she never orders anything."

Caleb chewed a bit longer. "Yeah, I'm surprised she came back to Jackson Grove at all."

"I'm not. As much as she hates this town, she's still royalty here. In her mind, it's better to be worshipped in hell than be a nobody elsewhere."

He swallowed as though the fluffy biscuit he'd been eating was month-old bubblegum. "But you don't see it that way."

"No, I like my place in town. I provide a needed service, and I'm at the point in my life where I'm comfortable being my father's daughter and not the debutante Mama wanted me to be."

"Your dad liked cars, too?"

"He's the one who showed me how to rebuild an engine." A twinge of pain throbbed in her chest when she thought about him. No one understood her like he had. "When he died, I used the money he left me to buy the shop. He'd always said my inheritance was supposed to be an investment in my future, and I couldn't think of a better use for it."

"Did he leave anything for your sister?"

"Of course he did. Kourtney also used her money to invest in her future, but instead of setting up a business, she spent it on a new nose, a new chin, and a new set of boobs."

Caleb stared down at his plate and played with the little bit of food left on it. "She had that much work done?"

"Would you like me to dig up pictures of her from high school?" Alex angled her face into his line of vision. "Don't act so surprised. A rack like hers is anything but natural."

"No, it's not that, it's just..." He threw his fork down. "You'd think she'd use it on something a little more meaningful."

"From her point of view, it was. Change her appearance until she's practically flawless, catch the attention of a hot guy with money, move far away from Jackson Grove. That was what she wanted for her future."

A wan smile tilted the corners of his mouth up. "And you think I'm the schmuck with money she was after?"

Alex paused, choosing her words carefully. "I can't answer for her."

"She must have mentioned something."

Now it was her turn to play with what was left on her plate. She could deliver the killing blow right here and end Caleb's interest in her sister, but if he left town now, it would end her chances with him, too. Besides, Kourtney was still her sister. "She mentioned that you came from a wealthy family and expressed some frustration that you refused to tell her why you wouldn't claim the trust fund your father left you."

"I'm surprised she even found out about it."

"Kourtney's smarter than most people give her credit for."

"No shit." He laid his fork down and pushed his plate away. "Just like your father, mine left us all a little something in case we needed it, but none us have except for Dan, who used it to pay off his med school loans. I may not be famous like some of my brothers, but I'm happy being a pilot. I feel like I'm doing something useful with my life, and I love flying. Besides, if I touched one cent of that trust fund money, I'd be kicked out of the Air Force."

"They'd kick you out for having a trust fund?"

He nodded. "When you come into that much money, the Department of Defense thinks your interests would be diverted from your duty."

Alex let out a low whistle. "That must be some kind of trust fund."

"It's enough to provide for a very comfortable retirement or maybe pass down to my kids someday. I don't need it. I make more than enough for my own needs. Hell, I'm still driving my dad's old car."

"Okay, first off, that 'old car' is a classic muscle machine that gets me hot and bothered just from listening to the engine."

"You get turned on by an engine?" he teased.

"Let me get behind the wheel and I'll show you." She gave him a playful nudge before turning serious. "Second, you should do what you love."

"Even if it's what made the woman I love leave me?"

A lump of bitterness rose into her throat. He was still in love with her sister. Alex took a breath, swallowed hard, and used those precious seconds to come up with a response that didn't incriminate her. "Being a pilot is who you are. You said it yourself—you love flying, and you loved it long before you met my sister. You shouldn't have to change yourself for another person. If you did, you'd only end up resenting that person later for taking you away from what you truly love."

He stared her with a line furrowed between his brows as though her words had hit him on a level he hadn't expected. She didn't understand why, though. To her, it was nothing more than common sense.

But then, most of the world lacked common sense. Herself included. After all, she was the one trying to lure her sister's ex into falling in love with her.

Thankfully, Miss Ada showed up to break the uneasy silence forming between them. "Y'all ready for dessert?"

Alex turned her attention away from the sexy man beside her and grinned. "Yep. Two peach cobblers, no ice cream on his."

"You sure about that?" Miss Ada asked Caleb as she took their plates.

"Positive." Once they were alone again, he said, "I'm surprised you remembered about my lactose intolerance."

"It's easy enough to remember, especially knowing what kind of discomfort it can cause you."

His expression sobered. "You'd think so."

Based on his reaction, she wondered how many times her sister had forgotten it.

Time to lighten up the mood. Alex slipped her arm

through his. "So, I'm thinking we act really cutesy over dessert and then end it with a kiss that will have those old biddies talking well into next week."

"How about I just put you on the hood of my Camaro and rev up the engine?"

She shivered from the thought of it. "Don't tempt me. I think Jackson Grove still has some public lewdness laws on the books that I'd be in danger of violating if you did that."

"And what we've done so far doesn't count?" He ran his hand along her thigh again, reviving that delightfully uncomfortable trickle of desire that flared to life whenever she got this close to him.

"Watch it, flyboy, or I may say screw dessert." *In favor of screwing me.* Her cheeks flushed, and she covered his hand with her own to keep him from tracing those little circles on her bare skin that made her sex ache. "This is a family establishment, after all."

His pupils dilated, and her heart kicked into overdrive. He licked his lips and leaned toward her. "Why don't we give those old biddies over there something to talk about now?"

Alex's breath quickened, but her mind issued a peal of warning. "Why?"

He backed away, blinking several times like she'd just decked him instead of asking a question. "Because it will get back to your sister faster."

All the heat between them vaporized, leaving behind a cold, sinking feeling. It was still about Kourtney. Alex pushed his hand off her thigh. "Let's just wait until after dessert."

An awkward silence settled over them until their peach cobbler was half gone and Caleb finally said, "I'm sorry."

"For what?"

"For dragging you into this situation."

"It was my idea, remember?"

"I know, but…" He tapped his spoon on what was left of his crust. "I came here so certain I'd succeed, but the longer I'm here, the more questions I have."

"Sometimes it's good to ask questions before making a big decision." *Maybe it will keep you from making a big mistake.*

"True, but…" He stabbed his spoon into the cobbler and pushed it away. "I just hope I find the answers sooner rather than later."

"Just stick to my plan, and you'll have your chance to talk to Kourtney by Wednesday."

"And what if I want to talk to her now?"

Panic gripped her stomach so tightly, not even Miss Ada's famous peach cobbler could entice her to take another bite. "Patience, Caleb. This is my sister we're talking about. Right now, she's still perfectly content with the son of the richest man in town. You need to make her jealous, to show her what she's missing out on if you want to have a chance with her."

His brows furrowed together again. "I just hate the idea of deceiving her. There's something wrong about lying to get someone to fall in love with you."

A new knot twisted in Alex's stomach. Considering that she was the one who'd sent all those emails to him, the last nine months had been one big deception, and she was at the heart of it. And even he did come to his senses about Kourtney, would he want her after learning about all the lies she'd been feeding him?

"Let's just go." She pulled out her wallet and left enough money on the table to cover the check and tip.

"I was going to pay for dinner."

"No, it was my idea." She rubbed her arms, wishing she could blame her sudden case of chills on the air conditioner that blasted through the café.

He slid out of the booth and offered his hand, but she didn't take it.

"Bye, Alex," Miss Ada called from behind the counter.

Alex gave a weak wave and headed for the door, fully aware of all the eyes that were following her.

Caleb caught her as soon as they were outside. "What just happened in there?"

She tried to shrug him off, but he pulled her back against his chest and wrapped his arms around her waist. She couldn't escape, but at least she didn't have to look him in the eye when she came clean. "You're right—we shouldn't have to conjure some huge deception to make someone fall in love with us."

He stilled behind her, the only movement coming from the rise and fall of his chest. Then he lifted her chin and used it to slowly turn her around. "Alex, I'm sorry."

"For what?"

"For asking you to be my wingman. For putting you between me and your sister. For upsetting you after you'd worked so hard on your plan to help me get her back."

She bit her bottom lip to keep from asking him why the hell he still wanted Kourtney. "It's fine, Caleb. I knew what I was getting myself into. Besides, who's to say my plan would've worked anyway? After all, why should you want me, especially after you've had her? They probably think you've lost your mind in there."

That same puzzled expression returned. "You think you're inferior to your sister?"

"Well, physically, yeah. I mean, I can't compete with her bazookas, much less anything else. She got all the looks."

"Oh, Alex, don't ever think that." He tucked a strand of her untamed red hair behind her ear and gave her a gentle smile that thankfully didn't contain an ounce of pity. "You are definitely a sexy woman in your own way."

"Yeah, if by sexy, you mean my ability to tell the make and model of a car by just the sound of its engine."

His grin widened until it crinkled his nose. "I find that very sexy."

"You're just saying that to make me feel better."

"Is it working?"

Her lips twitched. Caleb Kelly could charm the panties off a nun, but Alex couldn't help but notice the way he drew her closer into his embrace rather than maintaining that "just friends" distance she was all too familiar with. She wound her hands around his neck, watching for any sign that she was taking things too far. "Maybe."

"Then maybe I should keep going." He bent his head and kissed her.

Alex sucked in a breath and held it, wishing she could make this second last forever. Caleb's lips moved against hers, stripping past all her defenses and exposing that terrified core inside her. For a brief moment, she forgot that this was all for show. She indulged in the fantasy that he was kissing her because he wanted her, not because he was trying to give the town gossips enough fodder to make her sister jealous.

She decided to make the most of the moment. She released her breath with a moan and kissed him back, slipping her tongue into his mouth.

A hard ridge in his pants pressed into the softness of her stomach and emboldened her. Despite his declarations of love for Kourtney, Caleb couldn't hide the evidence of his arousal. She had the sign she'd been looking for. Hope intensified her desire. She dug her hands into the soft fabric on his T-shirt and rubbed against the hard planes of his body like they were lovers.

Caleb grabbed her ass and stopped the grinding, but he still kept her pressed against him. Now it was his turn to moan. He nipped at her bottom lip and pulled away with a shaky breath. "Do you think that was enough?"

A quick peek inside the café revealed that both Mindy and Mrs. Jefferies were back on their phones, this time with florid cheeks and rapidly moving mouths. "It got people talking."

"Good." But instead of letting her go, he kissed her one more time, although with less passion than before. "Let's stop before things get out of hand and they cite us for violating those public lewdness acts."

"Indeed." Right now, it was taking every ounce of self-control not to jump his bones. She pulled away and glanced down at his pants. Yes, there was still a hard ridge there, but it wasn't in the usual spot for a hard-on. She ran her hand over the bulge. "What do you have in your pocket?"

He looked away and gave her an embarrassed smile as

Falling for the Wingman

they walked down the sidewalk away from the café. For a split second, she worried she may have been mistaken and he had a really crooked erection. But then he slipped his hand into his pocket and pulled out a familiar figurine. "It's my good luck charm."

Alex's throat choked up when she recognized the angel she'd made shortly after she'd met Caleb. He'd let it slip that his call sign was "Crooked Halo," and she'd been inspired to create the little figurine out of spare parts and give it to her sister two Christmases ago. "Where did you get that?"

"From your sister. She gave it to me the Christmas before I deployed."

Alex dug her nails into her palms. Talk about re-gifting. She doubted Kourtney had kept it longer than a few hours before giving it away.

"I thought it was cute, what with my call sign and all." He stroked his thumb over the angel's face, and his voice grew quiet. "Now I truly believe it's a lucky charm."

The anger evaporated as she watched him stare with love at the collection of small metal bits she'd soldered together. "How so?"

"You know us pilots. We're a superstitious bunch. I took this with me so I could have a little something to remember Kourtney by and kept it in my flight suit. It wasn't until I barely missed getting hit by a SAM that I started to believe it was lucky. After that, it never left my pocket." To prove his point, he placed the figurine back into the safety of his pocket.

Part of her wanted to laugh from the absurdity of it all. When she'd asked for a sign, she'd never expected the

51

bulge in his pants to be the figurine she'd made. "Did she ever tell you where she got it?"

"I never asked. At first, I thought it was a little gag gift. You know, one of those things you find at a flea market for ninety-nine cents. Then I realized that the wings were a World War II–issued badge, and it started to grow on me."

She gave a bitter laugh. Maybe there was still some hope she'd grow on him.

"I'll ask her once I get her alone." He gave her a grin. "So, what's the plan from here?"

"Take it easy tonight. We've done enough to crank the gossip mill into high gear." *And tested my willpower enough, too.* "Tomorrow, come by the garage around five, and I'll take you over to Bubba's for dinner."

"Bubba's?" he asked, arching one brow.

"He and his wife are some of my best friends, and they're cooking some BBQ for us, along with J.T. and Mindy." She pointed back to the café to refresh his memory. "As you might recall, Mindy is one of Kourtney's best friends, and she's the maid of honor in her wedding."

"Why aren't you her maid of honor?"

Alex gave an unladylike snort. "We may be sisters, Caleb, but we're about as different as we can be. She's determined that I'm going to do something to ruin her wedding."

"Well, you technically are." He grinned.

"Getting you two together again aside, she'd been harping on me because I didn't have a date to the wedding. Then it was because I was refusing to wear a dress to the engagement parties and pre-wedding stuff.

Then it was because I refused to do something with my hair or wear makeup. In other words, I'm the troll marring her pretty little fantasy world."

He pressed his lips together in a tight line. "But you're still her sister."

"In your family, blood may be thicker than water, but in the Leadbetter household, it's all about appearances. And let's face it, I don't fit in with my mom and sister."

The line of his mouth thinned even more, but he dropped the subject and remained quiet until they returned to the garage. "So, back here tomorrow at five, huh?"

"Yep. And if tomorrow goes to plan, Kourtney will be tripping over herself to talk to you on Wednesday afternoon when we go to Mama's."

He nodded, and a hint of a smile played softened the hard lines of his mouth as he tucked one another stray strand of her hair behind her ear. "I'm glad you're not like them, Alex. You've always been so easy to be around, and I'm glad I can count on you to be my wingman."

Her eyes stung, and she turned away before he caught a glimpse of the moisture building in the corners. If she was so easy to be around, why did he still want her high-strung, self-absorbed, demanding sister? "Well, this wingman needs to get some shut-eye before tomorrow."

"Good idea. See you tomorrow."

She climbed the stairs to her loft above the garage but paused halfway up to watch him leave. He jogged back to his Camaro and fired up the engine, but he didn't leave right away. Instead, he rolled down the window and drummed his fingers along the top of the door, staring at her garage the whole time.

She held her breath. Maybe he was finally coming to his senses. Maybe he'd put two and two together and realized that she was the one who'd written the letters. Maybe he would turn the car off and come running up the stairs to take her to bed, saying he was finished with her sister and loved her instead.

But that never happened.

Instead, he turned the car around and drove in the direction of Miss Martha's, and Alex could no longer hold back the rogue tear that slipped out of her eye. She wiped it away. One tear. That's all she could bear to shed for Caleb Kelly right now. Tomorrow was another day, and if everything went to plan, she'd make some more progress in winning him over. And by the time he had his conversation with Kourtney, he'd realize her sister was not the woman for him.

CHAPTER FOUR

Alex grunted as she bent over the engine and pushed all her body weight against the socket wrench. The stubborn lug nut refused to budge. "Jermaine, I think we're going to need some WD-40."

The other mechanic handed her a can and grinned. "When you done loosening that tight bitch up, maybe we can use it on your sister."

"What are you talking about?"

Before he had a chance to answer, a woman's voice with a prissy Southern drawl came from the opening of the garage. "Alexandra, I need to speak to you in your office immediately."

Alex would bet anything that Kourtney was here to talk about Caleb, especially after their performance at the Sugar Belle last night.

Jermaine's grin widened as he hid behind the car's hood with her. "Just spray it between her ass cheeks, and maybe she won't be so high and mighty," he whispered before running over to another car.

It was tempting, especially after Alex peeked around the hood and noted the designer dress her sister was wearing. "I'm kind of busy with this engine at the moment."

"I don't give a horse's patootie what you're doing—my

business is far more important than yours. I need to talk to you about your recent behavior, and I'm not leaving until you promise that you'll stop embarrassing me."

Alex sprayed the lubricant on the lug nut and replaced the socket wrench. After one final shove, the nut loosened. She continued to work at it, never looking up from her work. "Let's face it, Kourtney, I'm always going to be an embarrassment to you, so there's no need to have this conversation again."

"Alexandra Leadbetter," her sister said with a stomp of her stiletto-clad foot, "you get your behind in your office right now."

"Whatever you want to say, you can say it to me here."

"I am not airing your dirty laundry where everyone in town can hear it."

"If you would come into the garage, you wouldn't have to shout."

"I'm not stepping foot in this filthy place. I'm meeting Mrs. McClure for lunch in ten minutes, and I refuse to get one speck of grease on me."

Alex laid the socket wrench aside and eyed the can of WD-40. It was tempting. So very tempting.

Jermaine returned. "You'd best let her get it out of her system because there ain't no telling what she'll do until she gets her way. I'll keep working on Miss Martha's car."

"Fine." Alex handed the socket wrench to him. "If I'm not back in five minutes, it's because one of us is dead and the other is trying to dispose of the body."

The other mechanic laughed and started working on the next stubborn bolt.

Alex stretched the kinks out of her back and pulled off

the black bandana she used to keep her hair out of her face when she was working, using it to wipe off some of the grease on her hands.

Kourtney wrinkled her perfectly shaped nose. "You are so disgusting."

"Want me to share?" She stretched out her dirty hand.

Her sister squealed and squeezed her Michael Kors purse to her chest. "Don't you dare touch me!"

Alex laughed and finished cleaning her hands before tossing the dirty bandana in the laundry basket. "Let's go to my office and get this over with so I can go back to work."

Kourtney followed her through the garage, still clutching her purse and contorting her body to ensure there was at least a good foot between her and anything she passed. "Have you ever considered hiring a cleaning lady for this place?"

"It's a garage, Kourtney. We fix cars. There's always going to be oil and grease everywhere." Alex caught a glimpse of herself in the window of her office. A black smear marred her cheeks, and her hair curled around her face like a frizzy halo. So very different from her sister, whose pale blond hair was teased and curled to fall in perfect ringlets.

She rubbed the smear off her cheek and collapsed into her chair. "Okay, let 'er rip."

Kourtney eyed the office with only a fraction less disdain than she had the garage. "I'm here to tell you to stop being the town slut and trying to seduce Caleb."

"Town slut, huh?" She rocked back in her chair. "Didn't that title used to belong to you?"

Her sister's lip curled into an unflattering snarl. "No, it didn't, but I can tell you what did belong to me—Caleb. And as far as you're concerned, he's still mine."

"And what does Ryan think about that?"

"That is no concern of his."

"I would think it is, especially since you two are getting married in a few days. Does he know he's the one you used to cheat on Caleb? I mean, if he's open to y'all being swingers—"

"Ugh! How dare you suggest something so vile! And I'd already broken up with Caleb before I started dating Ryan."

"Funny, because Caleb came home from Afghanistan thinking you'd be waiting for him."

"I left him a note."

Despite the fact they'd both shared the same lawyer father, it seemed Kourtney had never learned that anything she said could be used against her. "So, going back to the comment you made about having already broken up with Caleb, you admit that you two are no longer dating and that he's up for grabs?"

Her mouth opened into a perfect, red-rimmed circle before snapping shut. "It means he's up for grabs for anyone but you."

"Too late for that. I've been enjoying his company quite a bit." She gave her sister a suggestive grin, which only fanned Kourtney's ire. "Besides, you were the one who insisted I have a date for the wedding. I'm just grateful Caleb agreed to stay in town for a little fun."

Kourtney's surgically enhanced bosoms strained against her dress with every rapid shallow breath she took. "Now, you listen here, Alexandra. I ignored what I heard about your little performance at the Iron Line Sunday because I thought you were just distracting him long enough to get him out of town, but after last night, I have no doubt you're doing this out of spite. You will keep your hands off Caleb, and you definitely will not make a slut of yourself in front of everyone in town again. Do you hear me?"

If she'd just set out to make her sister jealous, she could count this as a success. But she wanted more. She wanted Caleb. "And what if *he* can't keep his hands off *me*?"

A blood vessel throbbed along Kourtney's neck. "I mean it. I won't have you taking what's mine."

"Then you should've thought about that before you left a great guy like Caleb because now that I have him, I sure as hell ain't letting him go." Alex rose from her chair. "Now, if you'll excuse me, I have work to do, and you have a luncheon date with your future mother-in-law."

Alex left her shock-eyed sister in the office and dived under the hood of Miss Martha's car, not caring how long it took Kourtney to pull her shit together and leave. Her whole life, she'd gone along with her older sister's demands because it had been much easier than trying to resist. But now she had something to fight for, and it felt good to finally stand up to her.

****

Caleb sat in his car down the street from the garage and stared at his good luck charm. He hadn't missed the flash of recognition in Alex's eyes when he'd shown it to her last night. For the last year and a half, he'd never wondered where Kourtney had gotten the figurine, but now it seemed to make sense. Alex had made it. It looked like something she would make, what with the leftover parts and the wry smirk on the angel's face. It matched her sense of humor.

He tilted his head back and groaned. Sleep hadn't come easy last night, and he wished he could've blamed the ache in his chest from the deep-fried Southern cooking he'd been consuming since he'd arrived in Jackson Grove. Instead, he knew who was to blame—Alex. He had no idea how it happened, but at some point last night, he'd forgotten about Kourtney and become all too aware of how tempting Alex was. Hell, he'd even called her sexy and meant it right before he'd kissed her.

This was seriously fucked up. He'd come here to win back his girlfriend, not hook up with her younger sister.

He checked the time on his watch. It was 4:56 p.m. Plenty of time for a quick call to gain some brotherly advice. He pulled out his phone and dialed Adam's number. "Got a minute?"

"For you? Definitely. Just give me a second." Part of a muffled conversation broke through, along with the crisp British accent of Adam's associate, Bates. Then Adam came back. "Sorry—I just needed to wrap up a few things."

"No problem."

"So I'm assuming this is about that woman you went to win back?"

"Yes, only..." Caleb's voice trailed off. In the last forty-eight hours, he'd begun to wonder if he'd ever known the real Kourtney. "Only now, I'm wondering if I

60

really want her back."

"Meaning?"

"I'm still in Jackson Grove, and I recruited her sister, Alex, to help me win her back by making her jealous." The ache in his chest returned. "But to be honest, I'm feeling a bit confused."

"You're not the only one. Care to enlighten me?"

"Well, first off, I get here to find out she's going to marry some other guy on Saturday."

"And you still want her back?"

"Two days ago, I would've said yes, but today, I'm not so sure."

"What changed?"

"Well, for starters, I'm actually enjoying hanging out with her sister. Alex gets me. She's laid back, no fuss, loves cars." *Is very easy to kiss and has me wishing this wasn't all part of an act.*

His heart thudded to a stop. *Holy shit! I'm falling for Alex.*

"Sounds like a winner. What's holding you back?" When he didn't answer, worry seeped into Adam's voice. "Caleb, are you still there?"

"Yeah, I am but…" He ran his fingers through his hair. "I think I'm in some serious shit here, Adam. On one hand, I still love Kourtney."

"Even after she left you for someone else?"

His throat tightened. The shock of her betrayal still stung, especially after all the things she'd said in her letters. But every time he read them, he was certain that was the woman he wanted to marry. "I wish I could explain what happened while I was away."

"Send me one of those emails you were talking about,

and Dan and I will run them through our bullshit analyzer. Hell, I'll even ask Lia for her assessment."

If the letters hadn't been so personal, he'd forward them in a heartbeat. "My problem is, I've been spending so much time with Alex that I'm forgetting about Kourtney."

Adam paused before saying in his most sincere voice, "Then maybe that's a good thing. She sounds like she's moved on. Maybe you should, too."

"But with her sister?"

"That's never stopped you before. Remember Lauren Riser in tenth grade?"

Caleb couldn't help but chuckle. He'd gone out with Lauren's younger sister, Bailey, then broken it off with her for her much older and more experienced older sister. The two sisters fought so hard to keep him that he'd been able to score with both of them before moving on to the next girl. "I am a little older and wiser now from that experience."

"Not to mention, having a few more notches in your belt. I never understood how you always had girls ready to hop into bed with you."

"Let's face it—I'm the most charming out of all of us." His laughter died, though, and he grew more somber. "I haven't slept with Alex."

"That's refreshing."

"No, I'm serious, Adam. I haven't, but last night, I came this close to following her to her place. The only thing that held me back was this overwhelming sense of wrongness. I'd feel like I was taking advantage of her, and she deserves better than that."

Another pause from his brother. "You know, I think this is the first time I've ever heard you turn down a chance to sleep with a woman."

"Well, technically, she didn't offer, but if she did, I still would've said no."

"Because she deserves better?"

"Yes." Caleb rubbed the center of his chest where the ache had returned with a vengeance. "Alex does. She's a girl I'd have no problem bringing home to meet Mom."

"Unlike her sister?"

Caleb pressed the heel of his hand to his temple as he remembered that disaster. His mother had come down to Florida a few months before he deployed and had taken an immediate dislike to Kourtney. "Yeah, I think even Mom would like Alex."

"Speaking of Mom, did you ever ask her why she hated Kourtney?"

"No." He'd been too angry at the time, too ready to defend his girlfriend and certain his mother had taken one look at Kourtney and dismissed her.

"Then maybe you should give her a call and ask that now before you propose to one of them."

"Hey, not all of us find our future wives after Mom bids on them for a charity auction."

Now it was Adam's turn to chuckle. "And for the first time in my life, I was glad Mom decided to play matchmaker. But seriously, she's a good judge of character, and maybe she saw something in Kourtney you'd been blind to."

"I'll think about it." He checked his watch again. It was 5:02 p.m. "I've got to run now, though. Another fake date with Alex."

"From what I'm hearing, there's nothing fake about them. Admit it—if you hadn't met Kourtney first, would you have fallen for Alex?"

Caleb didn't answer. Instead, he hung up to keep from admitting to his older brother how spot-on he'd been.

And to keep from admitting to himself that maybe he'd been chasing the wrong sister.

CHAPTER FIVE

"Hello, Caleb," Jermaine said with a wave as he entered the garage.

"Hey," he said, waving back, wondering how many people in Jackson Grove already knew his name after the past couple of days. "Where's Alex?"

"She went upstairs about fifteen minutes ago to get cleaned up. Said you was to go up and make yourself comfortable until she was done." The black man rolled a tire across the garage to the stack in the corner. "You should've been here earlier, though. You missed seeing Kourtney more pissed off than a drenched cat."

He paused at the staircase. Was Alex's plan working? "What do you mean?"

Jermaine grinned. "She had her prissy ass more uptight than usual on account of you and Alex neckin' all over town."

"We haven't been necking."

"That ain't what my mama said. She said you was more interested in Alex than dessert, and everyone in town knows how good my mama's peach cobbler is."

Caleb started putting two and two together. "Your mother is Miss Ada?"

"Yep. But getting back to Kourtney, she was yelling

and screaming at Alex to keep her hands off you or else."

Damn—Alex's plan was working. He'd gotten glimpses of Kourtney's jealous side while they were dating, but he'd never imagined she would threaten her sister. "And what did Alex say?"

Jermaine's grin widened. "Maybe you should let Alex tell you that."

"Tell him what?" Alex asked from the top of the staircase. She took a couple of steps and then turned to drag down a large ice chest behind her.

"Here," Caleb said, running up the stairs, "let me help you with that."

"Thanks." She waited for him to grab the other end and hoisted it up with him. "Bubba said to bring plenty of adult beverages."

"How many people is he expecting?" The cooler felt like it had about three cases of longnecks and enough ice to bury them in it.

"Just the six of us."

"And will we be able to safely drive back?"

"Probably not, but if that's the case, Bubba has a couple of guest rooms and a few tents."

His mind immediately went to sharing a tent with Alex after a few beers, to imagining what it would be like to share a sleeping bag with her, their naked bodies entwined. The blood rushed to his dick, and his grip loosened on the cooler.

"Hey, Earth to Caleb. I can't carry this on my own."

Alex's voice snapped him from his erotic daydream. "Oh, sorry." He lifted the ice chest high enough to cover his crotch and continued down the stairs. "I'm not sure we can fit this in my car."

"Not a problem since we're taking my truck." She steered him to the lot behind the garage and hoisted her end of the ice chest into the back of a classic Chevy pickup.

While she tied the chest down, he took a moment to admire the bright green truck. "What year is this?"

"A '57."

"What kind of engine do you have in it?"

Alex flashed him a mischievous grin. "One that's barely street legal."

"Nice." He climbed into the passenger side. "Let's see what this old girl can do."

"You got it." She started it up with a low, deep throttle that rumbled through the streets of downtown Jackson Grove. But when they reached the highway, she opened it and accelerated with enough power to knock him back against his seat.

Caleb rolled down his window and let the warm spring air whip past his face. The truck was a perfect combination of speed and power. "Let me guess—you built it?"

"Of course." The corner of her eyes crinkled from her proud smile. "Wait till you see what I have planned for that Roadrunner."

"Should my old Camaro be worried?"

"Most definitely." She chuckled and brushed the hair that had blown loose from her ponytail away from her face, her mood light.

Another thud of his heart bruised the inside of his chest. If he'd been riding with Kourtney, she would've yelled at him the moment he rolled down the window for messing up her hair. Alex, however, took it as a cue to roll down hers and enjoy the breeze too, not caring if her hair wasn't perfect.

She turned to him, and her grin faded. "Is something wrong?"

He shook his head. "I was just thinking about something. Do you want me to close my window?"

"Nope. I like driving down these old country roads like this." She turned off the highway to a small two-lane road that should have been repaved about three years ago. "Hang on—it's going to get a little bumpy from here out."

"Oh, I forgot—here in Alabama, most of the directions include 'Turn off the paved road,'" he teased. "I suppose mud-riding and cow tipping may be on the agenda tonight."

She stuck her tongue out at him. "We can put them there if you want. Just be thankful I didn't crank up my radio. I know how much you *love* country music."

"If I remember correctly, the last time we hung out, you were playing more classic rock." He grabbed the dash as a pothole jostled the vehicle. "That I can handle."

"You'll get plenty of that at Bubba's." She glanced at him, worry etching lines in her otherwise smooth forehead, and slowed the truck. "Here, I'll be more careful so you don't explode like a shaken Coke can."

"I appreciate it."

"And as for the beer, if you want, I won't drink tonight so we don't have to stay at Bubba's."

A stab of disappointment hit him. He'd actually been looking forward to sharing a tent with her.

Whoa! Watch it, Caleb. You're in danger of crossing the line, and she'd only end up getting hurt.

If she didn't slap him for trying to take things too far, that is.

"I'm okay with whatever."

Something flared in her dark brown eyes that made him wonder if she'd be more open to sharing a tent than he first thought. "Then we'll see how the evening plays out. In the meantime, I want you to relax, enjoy some good food and some great company."

"You're great company."

A hint of color rose into her cheeks. "Ah, thanks. You're good company, too, and I think you'll like my friends. We've all been like this since grade school." She held up her crossed fingers. "J.T. was in the Army, so you can rib him about that, if you want. And Bubba makes some of the best BBQ in the state."

"Just answer me one thing—is his name really Bubba?"

"Would you be shocked if I told you it was?" The twinkle in her eyes gave her away, but he shook his head, earning one of her unrestrained laughs. "Okay, you saw through that. His real name is Douglas Allen Grant III, but since his granddaddy goes by Big D and his daddy is Little D, his family decided to call him Bubba."

"Ah, the intricacies of Southern nomenclature."

She laughed again and gave him a playful nudge with her shoulder. "At least there's a dignified name on the birth certificate."

The road turned to gravel, and Alex slowed the truck down to a crawl. "We don't have much further, Caleb."

"I'm fine." The road cut through a thick forest of pine

trees. The afternoon light filtered through, making the coils of dust sparkle as the tires stirred them up. "This is actually kind of nice."

"I love coming out here. This land has been in Bubba's family for years. When they dammed up the Chattahoochee, it went from farmland to waterfront property."

"Farmland?" The moment the word left his mouth, the forest parted to reveal a flat grassy plain and a cottage-style home with a large wrap-around porch. Beyond that, the blue waters of a lake shimmered in the dying sunlight. "Nice."

"This is Bubba's."

As if he needed any clarification. A column of smoke rose from behind the house, filling the air with the mouth-watering aroma of hickory and roasted pork. His stomach growled. "I'm actually looking forward to this."

"You should because our little scheme aside, you deserve to have a good time and to relax and just enjoy being back home. My friends are all easygoing, so the only person you'd have to worry about putting on a show for is Mindy, and she and J.T. aren't here yet. Bubba and Lisa already know about my plan, so you can just be yourself around them."

Caleb exhaled, the last of the tension leaving his body. He liked the idea of just hanging out with Alex and her friends. If they were anything like her, it would be a laidback evening where he could forget about the craziness of the last three days.

Alex drove the truck around to the back of the house, where a couple stood around a smoker. The man was placing a kiss on the woman's cheek while his hand grabbed her ass. She gave him a half-hearted swat before turning around and waving at Alex and Caleb. "You finally made it. Bubba here was getting thirsty."

Alex turned off the engine and climbed out. "Sorry—I was working on Miss Martha's engine and forgot about the time."

"There's never an excuse for being late with the beer," Bubba teased.

Caleb got out of the truck, waiting for the awkwardness of being the outsider to set in.

It never did.

Instead, Bubba took his hand and shook it. "You must be Caleb. Alex has nothing but good to say about you, and I'm glad to finally meet you. Let me help you get that cooler down."

And just like that, he was part of the group. Alex introduced him to Bubba's wife, Lisa, and once they set the cooler down between the smoker and the empty fire pit, they all reached in and grabbed an ice-cold beer. Half a bottle later, he felt like he'd known them as long as Alex had. And even though they appeared to be simple country folks with accents to match, he was surprised to learn that Lisa was a nurse at the county hospital and Bubba was a paper engineer at the local mill. Both were well-educated and could find jobs anywhere, yet they seemed content to enjoy their life in this small town. It made him wonder if there was something about this place that kept them here.

Lisa got up from one of the lawn chairs around the fire pit. "I'm going to go inside and finish up the sides."

"Need any help?" Alex asked, rising from her chair

next to Caleb.

"Nope, I've got it. Why don't you take Caleb down to the lake and show him around?"

"Sounds good." She took his hand. "Come on—the water will feel good."

He finished off his beer in one quick chug and followed her to the narrow beach. The water was shallow enough to see the rounded rocks on the bottom for about ten feet out.

Alex took off her sandals and hopped from rock to rock with the grace of a ballerina. The short denim cutoffs drew his attention to her long, slender legs and her blue plaid button-down shirt tied at her waist, giving him a peek at her flat stomach. Her hair fell messily over her shoulders, the sunlight making the red and gold in the tousled waves burn like fire. She was the very image of a pretty country girl, but his thoughts were anything but innocent as he watched her.

He was thinking about how her legs would feel wrapped around his waist, about how silky the skin of her stomach would be as he ran his hands under her shirt to the gentle swell of her breasts, about how he'd love to tangle his fingers in her wild hair as he made her come. The haze of desire settled over his vision, and the blood rushed to his groin once again.

God help me, I'm not supposed to have these kind of thoughts about Alex.

But every time he tried to push them away, a new wave would ambush him. There was nothing intentionally coy or seductive in her actions, but the longer he watched, the more he wanted her.

She paused on a rock a few feet out, the water coming up to just below her knees. "Are you coming?"

He bit back a groan. He wanted to come, just not in the way she offered. He hadn't been laid since before he deployed, and judging by the hard-on she was giving him, it was nine months too long. If he didn't get hold of himself, he'd be asking Bubba for one of those tents so he could take Alex into the woods with him and find out if she lived up to the fantasies that were invading his mind.

Time for the equivalent of a cold shower. He slipped off his shoes and waded out until the cool water came up to his waist. The ache in his balls ebbed, but the lake did little to douse his thoughts about Alex.

"Caleb?" she asked, her voice rising with a hint of worry.

"Sorry, Alex." He splashed water on his face and forced those thoughts out of his mind. "I just needed to cool off."

"You kind of spaced out on me there." She came closer to him, stopping where the water lapped against the frayed edges of her shorts. "Are you not having a good time?"

The heat in his veins warned him that if she came much closer, he would be in trouble. He turned his back to her and continued to splash around until his T-shirt was as soaked as his shorts. "No, I'm having a great time. Almost too good of a time, actually."

"Then care to tell me why you bolted into the water like you were on fire?"

He pressed his palms against his temples. If he told her she was turning him on, how would she react? On one hand, she'd responded to his kisses like she enjoyed them

73

as much as he had. On the other hand, those kisses had all been part of their ploy to get people talking and make Kourtney jealous. Of course she'd act like she'd enjoy them. But until this J.T. arrived, they didn't need to put on a show. She'd said they could just be themselves. And right now, he was dying to know how she'd respond to his touch when they weren't performing for an audience.

Caleb turned around and closed the gap between them in three long strides. Without any warning, without asking for permission or testing to see how she'd respond, he pulled her against him and covered her mouth with his own.

She gasped, her body stiffening in surprise, and he mentally cursed.

Then her arms wrapped around his neck and her tongue dove into his mouth. She was kissing him back with a passion that matched his. Now it was his turn to stiffen in surprise, followed by releasing the moan he'd been holding back. He dragged her deeper into the water, never missing a beat. He wanted to drown in her kisses.

As if she'd known what he'd been fantasizing about, she wrapped her legs around his waist. Her fingers alternated between digging into his shoulders and running though his hair while her hips ground against his growing erection in a seductive dance that left him hating the layers of clothes between them.

He stumbled back, the water up to their chests, and finally came up for air. "Alex, if we're not careful…"

She pressed her finger to his lips. "Shh!" she hissed before kissing him again.

The knot tying the bottom of her shirt came loose, and

the fabric billowed around her chest, giving him the perfect opportunity to explore the silky flesh underneath. As he worked his way up along her ribs, he became painfully aware of her lack of a bra. He cupped one of her small breasts, and the ache in his cock intensified. But that was nothing compared to what the moan that rose from her throat when he rolled her nipple between his fingers did to him. That almost sent him over the edge.

Alex clawed at his T-shirt, bunching it around his shoulders until he was forced to end the kiss long enough for her to yank it over his head. Then she was on him again, her lips hungrily devouring his and leaving no doubt in his mind that this wasn't an act. She wanted him as much as he wanted her, and if they continued, a simple wade in the lake would turn into some X-rated skinny dipping.

She tilted her head back, exposing the lovely lines of her neck for him. As he tasted her sweet skin with a series of alternating nips and licks, he began fumbling with the tiny buttons of her shirt, determined to get her naked as quickly as possible.

He was working on the third one when a voice called out from the shore, "Hey, there's a law in this town against public indecency."

Alex jerked against him and snatched her shirt closed. A slew of whispered four-letter words spilled from her mouth before she shouted back, "We still have our clothes on, J.T."

"At the rate you two were going, I doubt they would've stayed on for long," he answered.

"Crap," Alex muttered and buried her head against

Caleb's shoulder. "I'm not sure if I should thank him for interrupting us or slap him into next week."

"Me, too." Alex was still in his arms, her legs wrapped around him, but her movements had stilled to the point where he could finally get control of himself. A few more seconds ticked by before he felt like it was safe enough to emerge from the water without a tent pole in his pants. "Should we get out and join the others?"

She unwound her legs, but didn't move away from him. "Are you okay?"

"Yeah, I think I am." He placed a quick peck on her forehead and carried her back to the beach, where the other couple waited for them.

Mindy looked like she'd just eaten a lemon as her fingers hastily typed a message on her cell phone, but J.T. gave them a wink. "When Lisa said you two had gone for a walk along the water, I didn't think I would stumble across you two going at it. If you two need a little more time alone—*ow!*"

J.T. rubbed his ribs after Mindy silenced him with a jab of her elbow. She glared at Alex. "Some people just have no sense of decency."

For her part, Alex didn't seem to be bothered by the other woman's hostility. She fastened up the two buttons he'd managed to undo and climbed out of the water. "Like I said, our clothes were still on."

Mindy narrowed her eyes. "I should've told J.T. to shut up until he could arrest you."

"Sorry, honey, but this is private property, and I'm off duty." J.T. kissed her cheek and offered his hand to Caleb. "Glad to finally meet you, Caleb. I'm J.T., and this is my

76

girlfriend, Mindy."

"Nice to meet you." He glanced over J.T.'s shoulder at the way Mindy stared down her nose at him. "And I've met Mindy before."

"Oh, yeah, I forgot you used to date Kourtney." J.T. flung his arm over Caleb's shoulder and dropped his voice to whisper as he led him back to the house. "And if you're just using Alex to get back at her sister, I swear to God I'm going to castrate you." He slapped him on the chest. "Just so we're clear on that."

He doubled back to his girlfriend, who was already whining about the heat and humidity.

Caleb stood where J.T. left him, wondering if he'd heard Alex's friend correctly. "Does he know about your plan?" he asked in a low voice.

Alex shook her head. "I didn't tell him because he'd blab it to Mindy."

"Gotcha, because he just threatened me."

She paused from wringing the water out of her shirt. "Why?"

"Seems he's worried I'm using you to get back at Kourtney."

"And are you?" She closed the space between them until her body was just inches from his.

"After what just happened between us, what do you think?" Never mind that her sister hadn't crossed his mind since he'd left the garage. All he could think about was the woman in front of him, and one of them was bound to get hurt if they didn't set some boundaries soon.

Her brown eyes searched his face, her expression unreadable. Then, ever so slowly, the corners of her mouth rose into a bittersweet smile. "That's up to you."

The air whooshed out of his lungs like she'd just punched him in the gut, and his feet remained rooted to the ground as she walked away. Was it all up to him? Was it as simple as choosing Alex over Kourtney? And if he did, would he ever forget about all those things her sister had written while he was deployed? Or would part of his heart still long for Kourtney?

CHAPTER SIX

Alex crossed her arms around her waist to keep from doubling over as she walked back to Bubba's house. *Why the hell did I do that?*

She'd had Caleb right where she'd wanted him. He was kissing her, caressing her, getting her hornier than a cat in heat, and J.T. had to interrupt him. Worse, she should've answered his question by reminding him of how good they were together, but instead, she'd seen that flicker of doubt in his eyes that morphed into a wall, clearly saying he wanted to keep some space between them. It didn't matter that she'd proven to him they had some seriously sizzling chemistry. As long as he wanted Kourtney, she would never be anything more than her little sister.

She entered the house, not glancing back once to see if Caleb was following. "Lisa, do you have some dry clothes I can borrow?"

"Of course." She turned around from stirring a pot of beans, and her lips curled into a frown. "What happened?"

"Caleb and I got a little carried away in the water."

"Uh-huh." She beckoned Alex to follow her to the master bedroom. "Care to talk about it?"

"Why not?" It had always been far easier to confide in Lisa than it had her own sister. She went into the master

79

bath, closed the door, and began shimmying off the wet shorts that clung to her body. "We were talking by the water, and the next thing I knew, one thing led to another."

Lisa handed her a T-shirt and a pair of loose-fitting khaki shorts from the other side of the door. "Who started it?"

"He did." She shivered as she remembered the way he'd grabbed her and kissed like a starving man. It was so rough, so desperate, so divinely erotic that she'd been helpless to fight it. Even when her mind warned her that she shouldn't give into him until she was certain he wanted her and not Kourtney, she couldn't resist the way his tongue danced around hers or the growing hardness of his erection.

And this time, there was no doubt in her mind it was his dick and not his good luck charm pressing against her.

"And?"

"And it was hot." She flung off her cold wet shirt that he'd almost gotten her out of and donned the T-shirt Lisa had given her. "Really hot."

"Then what's the problem?"

"It's just..." She paused with one leg in the khakis. "No matter how hot things are between us, I know he's still in love with Kourtney."

"Let's back up a minute. He's in love with your sister because of the emails he received from her while he was deployed."

"Uh-huh."

"The emails you wrote once you hacked her email address."

"Yep."

Lisa banged open the bathroom door and crossed her arms, her brows bunched together. "Then why the hell haven't you told him that you're the one who wrote them?"

"I was going to, but last night, he made this comment about how he hated using deception to get someone to fall in love with him, and—*bam!*—I chickened out because it was like he was accusing me."

"Do you think he figured it out?"

"No idea." Alex grabbed a towel from the linen closet and rubbed her hair with it. "There's a part of me that wants to see if given the right conditions, he'll forget all about her and fall for me, just as I am. No need to bring up those letters until afterward. I mean, you've read a few of those emails. Do you honestly think Kourtney would've said those things?"

"And what if you miss out on a chance for happiness with him because of your stubborn pride?"

"I'm not stubborn." She flicked the towel at her friend, even though the question still nagged at her conscience. What if she missed out on her chance with him because she was too scared to come forward with the truth? What if Kourtney snatched him back by taking credit for those emails?

"Aw, honey, you need to get your head on straight when it comes to him, and don't you dare sleep with him before then. It'll only confuse you even more if you do."

"I know, I know." Alex leaned back against the counter, her shoulders slumped in defeat. "It's just—you and Bubba have always been together. You've never had to live in Kourtney's shadow. You've never had guys dump you the moment they see her. And you've never had to win a guy over when he's in love with someone else."

Lisa hugged her. "Don't think about it that way, Alex. Remember, it's your words he fell in love with, and sooner or later, he'll realize that they came from your heart, not hers."

"And if he doesn't?"

"Then one of you is an idiot." She rumpled Alex's hair. "And if I hear he's marrying her and not you, you can sure as hell bet I'll be objecting at the wedding and giving him the cold hard truth. Of course, it'll probably end better if he hears it from you."

"I know. If things go to hell tomorrow, I'll tell him." Alex turned around and checked her reflection. "Do I look okay?"

"Fine, but I think you might've lost your bra in the lake."

"I didn't wear one." Not that it mattered. The only reason she needed one was to protect her nipples from a sudden chill in the air. Or the presence of one sexy, arousing man.

"And was that planned?"

Alex gave her a naughty grin that said it most definitely was planned.

"You're asking for trouble," Lisa warned with a matching grin.

"Well, if we end up staying the night, I'll make sure to pitch the tent some place where we won't keep you two up."

"Who's to say it won't be the other way around?" Lisa

scooped up Alex's wet clothes. "Let's get these in the dryer before you decide to get dirty again."

When they came back to the kitchen, Caleb was standing there with his shirt still off, giving her an ample view of his perfectly sculpted abs and pecs. His borrowed shorts hung low on his hips, a tempting trail of hair disappearing below the waistband. He met her gaze and stared at her with enough heat to make her skin flush. Sweet Jesus, the man was sex on a stick.

"Damn," Lisa whispered in her ear before nodding toward him. "If I wasn't married…"

"But you are."

"I know," she said with a sigh. "Can I help you with something?"

His eyes lingered on Alex a few seconds longer before he handed Lisa his wet shirt. "Bubba said I could toss this in the dryer, but I have no idea where it is."

"I'll take care of it." Lisa took the shirt and disappeared into the laundry room.

Alex bit her lip to keep from giving in to temptation and finding out where that trail of hair went. "You should probably put some bug spray on before going back out there, or the mosquitoes will have a feast."

"Yeah, Mindy hasn't stopped bitching about them."

"She's good at that." *Much like my sister.* "Lisa keeps the spray here."

Alex reached into the cabinet by the door and pulled out the canister, spraying his upper body and legs with the DEET mist before applying some to her own skin. "That should do it, especially since I see Bubba's already lit the citronella torches."

"Thanks." Caleb tucked his hands into his pockets and gave her a shy smile as he came closer. "Listen, Alex, about earlier…"

She held her breath. Was he going to tell her that he'd forgotten all about her sister and wanted her instead? Or was he going to apologize and tell her that it was all one big mistake?

Unfortunately, Lisa chose that moment to emerge from the laundry room. "I see Bubba's already pulling the pork," she said. "Time for me to get these sides out."

"We'll help take some out," Alex offered, her heart still beating irregularly from a few seconds before.

"Thanks, honey." Lisa slipped out the back door, leaving her alone with Caleb again.

She waited for him to finish what he'd tried to say, but instead, he grabbed the pot of baked beans. "So, are you ready to keep up the show for Mindy?"

Her heart slammed to a stop. They were back to acting like a couple to make Kourtney jealous. She faked a smile and shrugged to cover up her disappointment. "Sure."

She grabbed a bag of chips and followed him outside, wondering if she'd be better off spilling her guts and seeing where things went from there.

****

Caleb joined the others in on the chorus of "Sweet Home Alabama" and pulled Alex closer to him. A pile of empty bottles marked the progress of the night, and the campfire sent sparks dancing up into the clear, starry sky. After stuffing themselves full of the best BBQ he'd ever tasted, they'd lit the fire and passed around the ingredients for s'mores. J.T. had disappeared briefly to take Mindy home after she continued to complain about the "primitive conditions," but when he returned, he brought his guitar and led them all in a drunken sing-along. All in all, it was the best night Caleb had had in years.

And part of it was due to the woman sitting next to him on the picnic bench. Even though Mindy had left hours ago, Alex hadn't moved from her spot unless it was to get a soda. She'd stopped drinking when J.T. had returned, saying she needed to be sober to drive home, but she developed a delicious flush in her cheeks every time Caleb looked down at her.

Her fingers intertwined with his, pulling his arm tighter around her shoulders as she sang the last verse of the song with a huge grin on her face. An odd feeling of peace settled over him as he watched her. Here in her element, she burned as brightly as the fire in front of them, and it wasn't very hard for him to picture spending more nights like this with her. He was warm and relaxed, and his current state of bliss had nothing to do with the half-dozen beers he'd drunk so far.

Alex fit very well beside him. It left him wondering how well she'd fit with him in other situations.

And on the flip side, he wondered how well he'd fit with her. He glanced around the fire at her closest friends, feeling an instant camaraderie that he'd never felt with Kourtney's friends. These people were honest and easygoing, just like Alex. They accepted him for who he was and made him feel welcome. The night had been one of laughter and the occasional raunchy joke.

He liked Alex's world. Hell, he liked her. And more time he spent with her, the more natural it became to think of her as his.

The thought rocked his very core. The whole time he'd dated Kourtney, he'd worked so hard to keep her happy, to read her moods and keep her satisfied. But being with Alex was as easy as breathing. No guesswork. No trying to decipher the meaning of a pout before scrambling to fix it. No constantly watching what he said and did. Alex didn't put on airs like her sister. She was satisfied with her life in Jackson Grove, and it showed.

Now the only thing he feared was where he might fit in her life.

The strum of the guitar faded, and she lifted her head. "What time is it, Bubba?"

"Half-past drunk thirty with plenty more left to go in the evening." To prove his point, he fished another bottle from the cooler and opened it.

"I was being serious. Some of us have to work in the morning."

"Not me," Lisa said with a grin before swiping the open beer from her husband. "I'm in the middle of my three days off."

"And I'm calling in sick tomorrow." Bubba grabbed another bottle and tossed it to J.T.

"And I don't have to be on duty until noon."

"Slackers," Alex teased. She turned to him. "I think it's time we head out."

A twinge of regret dampened his spirits as Caleb rose from the bench. Then the beers hit him. He stumbled forward into Alex's arms, making no effort to leave even after he regained his footing.

"Are you sure you're safe to drive?" J.T. asked Alex.

"Do you want to administer a breathalyzer on me?"

"Nope, I'm off duty." He strummed an Eagles tune on his guitar. "Just be careful driving back. Aaron's on tonight."

"I'm completely sober."

Which was more than could be said for Caleb. The beer buzz was almost to the same level of intoxication as her kisses. He kept his hand around her waist, his mind flashing back to their misadventure in the lake. "Are you sure you want to leave? We can always borrow one of those tents."

And indulge in the fantasies that kept running through his mind.

She pressed one cool palm against his cheeks. "I think we'd better leave before you wake up with the hangover from hell."

At the rate he was going, he'd already be waking up in pain from a serious case of morning wood. He ran his hands down her back and along the curve of her ass. "But I'm having such a good time," he whispered in her ear, hinting that they could have a better time if they stayed.

But instead of agreeing to his suggestion, she backed away. That same flicker of pain filled her eyes, and the ache in his chest returned with a vengeance. "I'll go get our things from the dryer."

The whole night up until that point, there hadn't been an awkward moment with Alex's friends. But when she disappeared into the house, it came crashing down around him with enough force to chase away the pleasant warmth from the beer. He felt like a deer in the headlights as all three of them stared at him. The sweat prickling along the base of his neck had nothing to do with the warm humid night.

Lisa finally broke the silence. "It was nice to finally meet you, Caleb."

"Yeah, maybe we'll see you again," Bubba finished.

"Doubtful since I'm getting ready to PCS to Hill Air Force Base in Utah."

"That's too bad." Lisa's mouth curved down into a soft frown. "Does Alex know that?"

"I'm pretty sure she does." But did she? And if she did, would she come visit him? Or was she too rooted in her hometown to even consider leaving it?

Alex reappeared from the house wearing the same cutoffs and plaid shirt she'd arrived in. She handed him his T-shirt. "Ready to head out?"

He nodded and pulled the shirt on, his mood already sobered by the questions that filled his mind. "Need help with the cooler?"

"Nope." Bubba pounced on it. "This baby ain't leaving until it's empty."

Alex chuckled. "Just bring it back before the wedding. We'll probably need it for the reception."

If there was going to be a wedding. After all, that was the purpose of her plan, wasn't it? To get him back with Kourtney?

Yet the moment Alex took his hand to lead him back to the truck, he forgot all about her sister. He ran his thumb along the calluses of her palm and pulled her closer. The scent of the campfire lingered in her hair, mingling with the clean smell of fabric softener that rose from her still-warm clothes. It was everything that coming home should smell like, and he didn't want to let her go.

"Caleb," she murmured, "I can't drive with you holding on to me this way."

"Maybe because I'm trying to convince you to stay."

She looked up at him with a crease between her eyebrows. "Why?"

"Because everything feels so right here." He paused and added, "With you."

"You must really be drunk," she said, her soft laughter carrying a note of bitterness. "Let's get you back before you say something you regret."

He mulled over her words as they drove back into town. Was it just the alcohol talking? Or was he really entertaining the idea of a future with Alex instead of Kourtney? Perhaps it was time to start asking the hard questions. "This evening in the lake—was it all for show?"

She stared straight ahead at the road, but the way her hands gripped the steering wheel revealed her unease. "What do you think?"

"I'm still trying to figure that out. Did you know J.T. would catch us?"

"I knew he was coming, but I didn't know when."

The truck slowed as they came into town, and the familiar yellow Victorian came into view. He was running out of time. "Damn it, Alex, I need to know. Were you faking it out there in the lake or not?"

"What do you think?" she repeated before she pulled alongside the B&B and turned off the engine.

He was getting tired of this game. He needed answers, and he could only think of one way to get them. He unfastened her seatbelt and pulled her across the seat until she was practically in his lap. And when his lips covered hers, he got the answer he'd been searching for.

There was nothing fake about her kiss. It was the same raw, hungry, passionate eruption that rekindled his desire in a matter of seconds. Alex wanted him—of that he was certain. And God only knew how much he wanted her.

She straddled his thighs and continued to kiss him like she couldn't get enough of him. Her hips rocked against his hardening cock while her fingers raked through his hair. Every whimper, every touch, every flick of her tongue intensified the growing need inside him. If this was any indication, she'd be one hell of a firecracker in bed, and he wouldn't be content until he had her.

He found the buttons on her shirt and unfastened them enough to uncover one of her breasts. This time, he wanted to do more than just catch the taut peak between his fingers. He needed to taste every inch of her flesh.

Caleb cupped her ass and pulled her tighter against him, raising her up just high enough to where he could capture her nipple between his teeth. A sharp gasp came from her, followed by a moan that sent shivers through him and doubled the pounding in his balls. He drew the peak deeper into his mouth and was rewarded with another moan of pleasure, followed by a sexy whisper of his name.

Some long-buried part of his mind warned him to stop right there before things got out of hand, but he didn't want to stop until he was buried deep inside Alex. He yanked her shirt down past her shoulders, exposing both of her lovely breasts so he could alternate his attention from one to the other.

Her breath quickened, and the movements of her hips grew more erratic. Every time she said his name, it came out like a plea for him to continue. But as much as she seemed to be enjoying him, she stopped him cold by pressing her palm to his chest and saying, "Wait. Please, Caleb, I…" Her voice trailed off as she struggled for air. "I need to know that this isn't all for show, that you want me for me and not because you're trying to keep the rumor mill alive."

He guided her hand down to the erection that strained against his zipper. "Does this feel real to you?"

She ran her finger along the length of his cock, sending a series of tiny shocks through him with every inch. Uncertainty still lingered in her eyes. She bit her bottom lip and drew in a deep breath. "Say my name, then."

"Alex." Her name came out like a feral growl, and he buried his face in her hollows of her neck, pressing his lips over the point where her pulse throbbed. "I want you, Alex. I need you. Now."

The last of her resistance faded, and her body melted against his. She was giving him permission to continue, to quench the raging desire welling up inside. He wanted to bury himself in her over and over again until they both went over the edge. He wanted to hear her scream his name as she came.

Her fingers found their way to the waist of his shorts, undoing the button and pulling down the zipper. His cock sprang free, only to be wrapped up in her hands. A haze of lust settled around him. She stroked the length of his erection while nibbling on his ear and pausing to occasionally say his name in a sexy voice that almost made him come each time she used it.

And if he didn't get her naked soon, he was going to be coming much sooner than he would've liked. He almost had no restraint left.

It's been so long, so very long…

Alex froze, then pulled away. "What was that?"

The shocking chill doused the fire in his veins and bought him crashing back to reality.

Dear God, what had slipped out?

****

Confusion followed by panic washed over Caleb's face after Alex asked her question. Yes, she'd heard him correctly. She looked away and pulled her shirt back on.

He reached for her, but she retreated to the driver's seat, adding some much-needed space between them. "Alex, what just happened?"

A sharp pain filled the hollows of her chest, chasing away the heated desire that had set her on fire just moments before. He'd said he wanted her, but then the real reason why had slipped out. Bitterness seeped into her soul and spilled out into her voice. "So, how long has it been since you got laid? A few months? A year?"

He said her name like a desperate apology, but she cut him off before she fell for his games again. "No, Caleb. If this is going to happen between us, then I need to know it's because I'm something more to you than just a quick fuck."

"You are." He slumped in the passenger's seat, his gaze fixed on the roof of her truck. "Would saying I'm sorry help?"

She gripped the steering wheel to keep from jumping

back into his arms. "I'd rather hear it from you when you're sober."

He winced. "So there's no chance we could continue this upstairs?"

She gritted her teeth and stared straight ahead. Her body was still clamoring to pick up where they left off, but her bruised heart couldn't bear anymore. "No, not tonight."

"Then can you at least take me back to your place so I can get my car?"

"Nope. You heard J.T.. Aaron's on tonight, and he's the biggest asshole on the force. He'll jump at a chance to pull you over for a DUI, especially with your Illinois plates."

"Then what's going to happen to my car?"

"It'll be safe at my place until tomorrow. You can walk over around lunchtime and pick it up then."

A rustle of movement earned a sideways glance from her. Caleb was zipping his shorts back up, all evidence of his arousal gone. "For what it's worth, I am sorry, Alex."

Her eyes burned. *Yeah, me too.* But she said nothing as he got out of her truck and walked up the pathway to Miss Martha's B&B.

Minutes ticked by before she finally started the truck back up and drove home. Her mind warred with itself. Maybe she'd made a mistake. Maybe she'd dodged a bullet. Maybe she was nothing more than the queen of lost causes. It didn't matter. Because as perfect as tonight had been, she still hadn't won Caleb's heart.

At least this will be over by tomorrow, she told herself as she climbed the stairs to her loft. Tomorrow, Caleb would have his chance to talk to Kourtney, and they'd go from there.

CHAPTER SEVEN

Caleb rolled over and immediately groaned. It was bad enough his sleep had been total shit last night, with the constant throbbing in his balls reminding him how he'd royally fucked up with Alex. Now the damned sun threatened to take the current throbbing in his head to a whole new level. Adding to his agony was an additional pounding from the door.

"Yoo-hoo, Caleb, darlin', time to wake up," Miss Martha's overly cheery voice called from the hallway.

He cracked open one eye and spied the alarm clock on the nightstand. 10:39 a.m. No, it wasn't time to get up. He wanted to sleep all goddamn day until he figured out what the hell he was going to do next.

"I need to get your room ready for the next guest," she continued. "Do I need to come in and drag you out of bed?"

The doorknob jiggled, and his heart jumped into throat. He bolted to the door to keep the B&B owner from barging in and discovering how easy it would be for her pinch his bare ass. "I'm up."

Unfortunately, the contents of his stomach threatened to follow the same path as his still-racing heart. He covered his mouth and prayed he wouldn't puke.

"All righty," Miss Martha sang in a voice that was way too chirpy for his ears. "Checkout time is eleven. I'll fix a cup of coffee for you."

The fading sound of footsteps eased the tension from his muscles, and he sank to the cool hardwood floor, still leaning back against the door. It was Wednesday, the day he was supposed to get answers from Kourtney. Where had the week gone? And more important, did he still want those answers?

He closed his eyes and tried to remember how Kourtney had felt in his arms, but all he could think about was Alex. The softness of her hair. The hint of vanilla on her skin. The fire in her kisses. What would have happened if those drunken words hadn't slipped from his mouth? Would sex with her be everything he'd imagined? Or would it have been an awkward mistake that would forever haunt him?

One thing was certain—he needed to clarify where he stood in regards to the two sisters, and right now, his mind was as clear as mud. He forced himself to his feet and stumbled to the shower, letting the warm water wash away the fog that surrounded his mind.

By the time the clock read eleven, he was packed, dressed, and feeling a bit more coherent. The aroma from the steaming black coffee Miss Martha handed him when he came downstairs chased away the last remnants of sleep. "How much do I owe you for the room?" he asked before taking a sip.

"Not a penny," she said with a grin. "Alex and I worked out a deal for your room."

Crap. One more reminder of how Alex had gone above

and beyond to help him out. "I enjoyed my stay and wish I didn't have to leave."

"Oh, I do too." She cast an appreciative glance at his backside. "But I have a feeling you'd have no problem finding a place to stay until the wedding, especially judging by the way you and Alex fogged up the windows of her truck last night."

He paused, the coffee cup hovering an inch above his mouth. Jesus, didn't people in this town have anything better to do than spy on him and Alex? When Alex had told him they would have tongues wagging, she wasn't kidding. He cleared his throat, not wanting to disclose how the action in the truck ended on a sour note. "We'll see."

"Save a dance for me at the wedding." She gave him a girlish wave and headed up the stairs.

Caleb took his bag out to the oversized front porch and sat on the swing to finish his coffee before heading to the garage. He needed to figure out what he was doing before he faced either Leadbetter sister. He pulled out his phone to ask Adam for more advice, but his finger continued down his contact list to his mom's number. Perhaps it was time to learn the hard truth.

"Caleb, sweetie, I was wondering when you'd call."

He bit back a groan from the heavy guilt trip her words carried. "Sorry, Mom, just been busy with things."

"I'm just glad you're safe and back home. And speaking of home, will you be coming to Adam's wedding in a few weeks?"

"I've already contacted my new CO at Hill and asked for the weekend off."

"Wonderful! I can't wait to see all my boys together again."

He stretched out and leaned back in the swing. "Speaking of Adam, has he told you what happened when I came home?"

"No," his mother said in a careful voice that revealed her lie. "Care to tell me?"

"Not really." Besides, it sounded like she already knew most of the details. "What I'd really like to know is why you didn't like Kourtney when you met her last year."

"Caleb, I really don't think—"

"Mom, I want the truth. Don't hold anything back."

A pause filled the line. "I know you were crazy about her."

"I was, but now I'm starting to see a different side to her, and I value your opinion."

Another pause, followed by a sigh. "I'm not surprised she left you, Caleb. She was probably the most self-absorbed person I've ever met, and I got the distinct impression she was more interested in what our family could do for her than she was in you. For example, she asked if I could pass on a photo of her to Gideon's manager to see if it would get her an audition in Hollywood. And the whole time I was there, she kept saying how she hoped you'd be reassigned to Nellis so she could enjoy the nightlife in Las Vegas. I can only imagine how disappointed she was when you got Hill instead."

He let his mother's assessment sink in. So far, it matched what Alex had let slip out. "Then you'll be happy to know she left me while I was deployed. In fact, she'll be marrying someone else in a few days."

"Yes, but Adam told me you're in her hometown to win her back. Are you sure you still want her?"

He rubbed the side of his face. Sunday, he would've said yes in a heartbeat. But now, after spending so much time with Alex and discovering the explosive chemistry between them, he was left wondering the same thing. "I'm supposed to have a chance to talk to her today. Maybe after that, I'll have a better idea what happened."

"As you wish." Which was his mother's way of saying that she thought he was making a huge mistake. "I don't suppose you'll have to time to come up to Chicago on your way to Utah?"

"We'll see." If everything blew up in his face this afternoon, he'd have a few days on his hands.

"Okay, sweetie."

"Mom, I'm not three anymore. You don't have to call me 'sweetie.'"

"Nonsense. You're all still little boys to me."

A new wave of nausea threatened to overtake him. "I need to get going. I promised Alex I'd meet her at the garage before heading over to Kourtney's mom's house."

"Alex?" Her voice rose a bit higher with curiosity. "Who's that?"

Adam's question about taking Alex home to meet Mom echoed through his mind. "Maybe you'll find out."

That is, if I haven't royally fucked things up with her.

"It's not nice to tease your mother, Caleb."

"Good-bye, Mom."

"Bye, sweetie." She drawled out the last word as though it were payback for not telling her about Alex.

He ended the call and finished his coffee, wondering

what else Kourtney had said to his mother when they met last year.

Remember the emails. Just ask her about them, and go from there. If she meant what she said in them…

Crap. Was it too much to hope Kourtney was lying?

****

Alex was bent over the engine of a late-model Town Car when Caleb arrived at the garage. She was so focused on her work, she didn't notice him, but Jermaine gave him a friendly wave from the interior of the car.

"All right, I think we've got it." Alex straightened and wiped her hands on a rag. A few damp curls had slipped out from under her bandana to frame her face, and a streak of grease on her jaw did little to detract from her appearance. She looked as sexy to him as she did last night. "Start her up."

The engine roared to life and settled into a contented idle.

Caleb came alongside and assessed her work. The engine looked like it had been completely rebuilt and rumbled like a car fresh off the lot. "Not bad."

She gave him a proud grin and lowered the hood. "She may not look like much, but in the right hands, she can purr."

I'd love to make you purr. The rogue thought ambushed him with such intensity, he had to turn away before she guessed his thoughts. Yep, he still wanted her. The question was—did she still want him, especially after last night's gaffe?

"How's your head this morning?" she asked, her eyes never leaving his face.

100

"Fair enough." He shifted the bag on his shoulder. "Listen, Alex, about last night—"

"I've got to get cleaned up before heading over to Mama's." She threw her rag in the laundry bin and started for the stairs. "You're welcome to come upstairs in the meantime."

She'd just dissed him. Not a good start to the morning. "Okay. I'll just put my stuff in the car first."

When he came back into the garage, Jermaine and the other mechanics all watched him with smiles of barely contained laughter. "Am I missing something?" he asked them.

Jermaine finally erupted with a chuckle. "I don't know what you did, but you're in the doghouse with Alex."

"No shit. And I take it you're enjoying every minute of it."

"More like I can't wait to hear what happens when you get stuck in the middle between Alex and Miss Tight-Ass Kourtney." He rubbed a smudge off the Town Car Alex had been working on. "I ain't ever heard of the two of them fighting over a guy, but I reckon there's a first time for everything."

"So I'm not completely in the doghouse?"

"She invited you upstairs, didn't she?" Jermaine gave him a wide grin that looked just like his mother's. "I'd better get this car back over to Miss Martha. Want to come along?"

Caleb stuffed his hands into his back pockets. He'd escaped without a pinch this morning, but he'd only be pressing his luck if he went back. "Nah, thanks, though. I'd better head upstairs before I make Alex late."

"Good idea. Kourtney pissed off is bad enough. You throw in Miss Lizzie, and we're talking one major shit storm."

"Thanks for the warning." He bounded up the stairs and opened the door to Alex's apartment above the garage. Steam billowed out from under the bathroom door, and his thoughts turned to Alex in the shower, of her running her hands over her naked skin, touching herself, getting all warm and wet...

His dick started hardening, and he shook the thoughts from his head before he decided to act on them and join her. As much as he physically wanted Alex, he owed Kourtney a chance to explain herself. And he needed to know the truth about the letters that had made him fall in love with her because if she'd truly meant what she'd said, then he had no business cheating on her with Alex.

He wandered over to the partially refurbished Roadrunner and spent a few moments admiring it before noticing the small workbench off to the side. A divided tray of spare watch parts and gears next to a soldering iron caught his attention. He pushed it aside to reveal a compartment underneath with more than a dozen tiny figurines made from those spare parts.

He pulled out his lucky charm and compared it to the others, noting the similar craftsmanship. None of them had the same expression or the wings, but they were similar enough to all come from the same artist. He squeezed his lucky charm in his palm and grimaced.

Well, that was one question answered. Alex had made the angel with the crooked halo, not Kourtney, and she was the one he needed to thank for saving his life. Was she responsible for anything else?

"See something you like?" Alex asked behind him.

He turned around to find her standing a few feet away wearing nothing but a towel. The need to touch her threatened to overtake his better judgment, but he managed to keep his desire in check as he held up his lucky charm. "You made this, didn't you?"

After a pause, she nodded.

"Why didn't you tell me the other night?"

"Would you have believed me?" A flicker of anguish passed across her face before she fixed a tight smile in place. "I'll be ready in a few minutes."

She turned to go back to the living room, but after a coy glance over her shoulder, she let the towel pool around her ankles and continued toward her bedroom completely naked.

Caleb tightened his grip on the lucky charm until the metal wings dug into his palm. *Dear God, does she have any idea what she's doing to me?* It was torture to watch her walk away, her damp hair swishing just above her bare ass, and not chase after her. The desire he'd felt last night returned with a vengeance that nearly brought him to his knees. But her words from last night kept his feet fixed in place.

If this is going to happen between us, then I need to know it's because I'm something more to you than just a quick fuck.

And until he straightened out the matter of the emails, his heart was still bound to her sister.

****

Alex held her breath and focused on copying the seductive sway of her hips that she'd seen her sister employ numerous times. When Kourtney walked away, men followed like greyhounds chasing after that mechanical bunny. But when she walked away, the one man she'd hoped would follow stayed right where he was.

Figures.

She'd hoped that once she confirmed she'd made the angel figurine, he'd put two and two together and ask about the emails. But he didn't. Hell, he didn't follow her into the bedroom when she'd openly invited him to finish what he'd started last night.

Let's face it. You blew it, and you're going to have stand back and watch him continue to make a fool of himself over Kourtney.

Or just come clean with everything. But if she told him now, would he believe her?

She yanked a clean pair of jeans from her drawer and pulled them on, frustration punching out her movements. Unless Kourtney lied to him when he confronted her about the emails, he'd learn the truth. Then she'd come clean.

She just hoped Caleb wasn't stupid enough to fall for her sister's lies.

She finished dressing and came out of the bedroom to find Caleb just as she'd left him, still standing in the same place and clutching the angel figurine in his hand. "You okay?"

A hint of indecision flickered in his eyes, and he glanced down at the figurine. "Yeah, I'll be fine once I get this over with."

A new jolt of pain ripped through her chest. He probably couldn't wait to end their fake romance so he could get back to her sister. The sad thing was, every once in a while, she almost believed it was real, that Caleb could actually fall for her. Unfortunately, that kind of ridiculous hope made reality ten times more harsh when it came crashing down around her.

She buried her grief deeper inside. "Come on, then. The sooner you have your rendezvous with Kourtney, the happier you'll be."

"Alex, wait." He caught her hand before she reached the door and took a deep breath. "I'm sorry about last night."

"You were drunk." She tried to slip her hand free, but he held onto her as tightly as he did his good luck charm. "Really, Caleb, it's nothing."

"Yes, it is. I know I said something to hurt you, but that wasn't my intention." He released her and looked around the room, his shoulders slumped. "In fact, nothing this week has gone the way I'd intended."

"Don't say that. I know for a fact Kourtney's madder than a hornet about our little escapades, and she'll probably pounce on you the first moment she gets. You'll see."

"Maybe." He looked down at the figurine one more time before stowing it back in his pocket. "But back to what I said last night—what I was trying to tell you is that I was so out of practice, I worried I'd come before I'd given you what you deserved."

Her breath caught, and that familiar warmth of desire stirred within her lower stomach. "And what's that?"

The sexy glow returned to his eyes, and he gave her a crooked smile that intensified the throbbing of her heart. "I wanted to make you come. Multiple times, in fact."

Then, just as quickly as it appeared, Caleb's flirtatious

side vanished. "But I'm glad you stopped things before they got out of hand. You deserve better."

Her tongue refused to move. It would be so easy to wrap her arms around him and drag him to the bed with a searing kiss, but it would be no different than last night. She wanted to be more than a quick fuck. She wanted the whole package. And maybe, just maybe, his meeting with Kourtney today would be enough to tip the cards in her favor.

She licked her lips and found her voice. "I promised to play your wingman this week and get you close enough to Kourtney to find out what happened. Let's not miss what we've worked so hard for by being late."

"You've been the best wingman I could've hoped for."

"Good, because I'm in this for the long haul. Whatever happens, I just want you to be happy." She grabbed her phone and wallet and ran to the door before he had a chance to stop her again. "Let's go before the catered lunch disappears."

"Fine, but we're taking my car."

At least there's a silver lining to this, she thought with a rueful grin. She'd finally get a ride in his Camaro.

CHAPTER EIGHT

By the time Caleb pulled into the Leadbetters' driveway, his stomach was roiling, and he only wished he could blame it on last night's beer.

Alex hadn't said anything to him on the way over, which was a small blessing. He'd already let his dick get the better of him and said more than he'd wanted at her place. He'd let her know he wanted to sleep with her, which was an asshole thing to do considering why he was here. And to her credit, she had enough composure to keep focused on his mission and prevent him from making another possible mistake.

In other words, she was being the ideal wingman.

Worse, he knew he was hurting her, despite her attempts to hide it from him. He'd seen it in the way her mouth angled down and the pinch in the corners of her eyes. But he owed it to himself and to her to find out what had happened while he was gone. Once the facts were clear, then he could move forward.

Alex hopped out of the car as soon as he threw it in park and went straight for the front door. He managed to catch up just as she reached the foyer and Kourtney appeared from the doorway of the other room.

"You're late," she said, her eyes narrowed. Then

107

Kourtney saw him, and her expression did a one-eighty into shock. "What's he doing here?"

"He came to help out." Alex took his hand and led him to the same room he'd run into on Sunday. Only now, instead of being filled with Kourtney's future in-laws, it was packed with bridesmaids, all of whom stared at them as they entered. Alex appeared to ignore them and went for one of the boxes of wedding favors. "What do you need us to do?"

"I need you to start filling the bags with Jordan almonds, and I need him to leave. Now."

He'd always known Kourtney liked to be in control, but she was taking things to a whole new level of bitchiness. "I'll just hold the bags while Alex fills them."

The glare she shot at him contained only half the fury of the one she directed toward Alex. Her nostrils flared and she curled her fingers so her painted nails looked more like claws.

An overwhelming urge to protect Alex took over, and he moved between the two sisters. "Relax, Kourtney. We're not here to make any trouble."

Her mouth opened and closed a few times before she spun around in her high heels and retreated to the furthest corner from them.

"That went well," Alex murmured as she pulled a box of pastel coated almonds down from the stack. "Give her a couple of minutes to cool down."

"And then?"

Alex gave him a conspiratorial wink. "Then you can fetch me a Coke from the fridge, maybe even help yourself to some of the sandwiches I know are in the kitchen."

"Sounds like a plan."

And as he held open the little pink bag for her to scoop the almonds into, he realized that Alex had been right about everything. Every time he glanced toward Kourtney, she was staring at them with a mixture of anger and jealousy. Alex had set up the perfect plan of attack, and it was up to him to carry it out.

It was now or never. He leaned over to place a kiss on Alex's cheek. "Wish me luck," he whispered before saying in a louder voice so Kourtney could hear, "I'm going to grab something to drink. Care for anything, Alex?"

"Just a Coke." She continued filling the little bags with candy, but when she looked up from her work, he saw the same anxiety that flowed through his veins on her face. She gave him an almost imperceptible nod and went back to the candy.

Caleb wandered across the room, checking just once to see if Kourtney was watching. When he got the confirmation he needed, he disappeared into the kitchen and zeroed in toward the fridge for the sodas. He'd barely had a chance to grab two before the door to the hallway slammed shut. He turned.

Kourtney stood in front of him, her arms crossed. "What the hell do you think you're doing, Caleb?"

"Getting a soda for me and your sister." He held up the cans as evidence.

"That's not what I mean, and you know it." She snatched the cans from his hands and slammed them on the counter. "I'm not amused by your little rebound fling with Alex."

"Says the woman who left me while I was deployed and

hooked up with another man." He stuffed his hands into his pockets, his fingers brushing against his good luck charm, and leaned against the fridge. "Care to explain to me what happened while I was away?"

"Only if you agree to stop making an ass of yourself with Alex."

"Jealous?"

"Hardly." But he didn't miss the flare in her eyes as she raked her gaze up and down his body. "Just what are you doing here in town?"

"I came here for answers."

"You saw the day you arrived that I'd moved on."

"And maybe I have, too." That caught him by surprise. Maybe Alex was just what he needed to get him over the sting of Kourtney's rejection.

"That doesn't explain why you're still here."

"I told you why I'm here. And besides, Alex needed a date for the wedding, and I'm having a good time with her."

"Is she aware that you're only fucking her to get back at me?"

The slap of her words almost shattered his patience. He straightened up and closed the space between them. "Who says I've slept with her?"

"The whole town is talking about what a slut she's being."

Once again, the urge to protect Alex took over. He backed Kourtney against the counter and imprisoned her by placing his hands on the counter on either side of her. "You shouldn't talk about your sister that way."

"Then leave before you ruin both my wedding and her

reputation."

"Not until you answer a few questions."

Her bottom lip quivered, but she arched one haughty brow. "What?"

"After I deployed, how many days did you wait before you moved back here?"

Her breath quickened, and her anger gave way to panic. "Maybe a week. I couldn't handle being alone."

"And were you hooking up with your fiancé the whole time you were sending me those emails?"

"Emails?" Her perfectly groomed brows drew together. "What are you talking about?"

"The emails you sent me while I was deployed."

"The only letter I wrote to you while you were gone was the one you found in our apartment, in which I made it very clear I wanted to be with someone who wouldn't abandon me for months at a time."

Now it was his turn to do the one-eighty into shock. "If you didn't send me those emails, who did?"

"Are you sure you didn't inhale any hallucinogens while you were over there? I have no idea what emails you're talking about, but I can assure you, they didn't come from me. My email got hacked right after I returned home, and I had to get a whole new account."

He backed away, still trying to digest this new information. She'd just denied the one thing that had bound his heart to her, and now it was free. But it still didn't solve the mystery of who was behind the emails. They might not have come from Kourtney, but he was starting to get a good idea who they might've come from. There was still one woman who knew him better than he knew himself, who could put his soul at ease, and whose kisses felt like coming home.

Kourtney inched away from him. "Now that I've answered your questions, will you please leave town so I don't have to worry about you ruining my wedding?"

"So you're serious about this guy?"

She swallowed hard and nodded. "Like I told you, I'm not cut out to be a military wife. I wanted more than you could give me."

"Then I'm glad you found someone who could give you what I couldn't." He took the two cans of soda. "I'll take these for the road."

When he returned to the front parlor, he found Alex watching him with the same uncertainty and fear he'd glimpsed in her so many times since arriving in Jackson Grove. Now it was time to put her mind at ease. He was finally able to put Kourtney behind him and move forward. "Let's go, Alex."

"Where?"

"I don't care." He tossed her the keys to his Camaro. "You get to drive, though."

Her face lit up like a kid's on Christmas. "You're letting me get behind the wheel?"

"Yep. It's time we start fulfilling some of those fantasies of yours." And do it without the whole town spying on them.

Kourtney stormed out of the kitchen. "Now wait just one minute. I told you to leave, Caleb, but I need Alex here to finish my wedding favors."

"No, you don't. You made it quite obvious you think Alex's presence is more of a hindrance than anything else,

112

and I think she deserves to be treated better than that." He stepped between the two sisters again and ushered Alex to the door. "Your chariot awaits."

Alex dashed for the door, the keys jangling in her hands.

He turned around and gave Kourtney an honest smile. "Thank you. You've just kept me from making a huge mistake."

"And yet you're still determined to ruin my wedding, aren't you?"

"Not at all. I'm just going to let Alex have some much-deserved fun." He started backing toward the front door. "Maybe I'll stick around long enough to see you walk down the aisle and wish you well."

But right now, all he cared about was seeing where things went with the one woman who revved up his heart like a classic muscle car engine.

****

I must be fucking dreaming.

Alex ran her hand over the steering wheel and pressed the gas a few more times. The Camaro vibrated with a sexy growl that was even more powerful than she'd imagined. The hairs on her arm rose in excitement, and butterflies danced in her stomach.

Caleb hopped into the passenger seat. "How far away is Atlanta from here?"

"One and a half, maybe two hours, depending on traffic. Why?"

"Because you and I are going to have a night out on the town." He pulled out his phone. "I thought you wanted to see what this car can do."

"I do, but I'd rather know what you're up to." *And what my sister said to you in the kitchen.*

"Just drive while I make a few calls."

"Yes, sir." She slipped her Bluetooth headset into her ear and threw the car into reverse. The car shot out the driveway like a cannon. A minute later, she was flying down the two-lane highway out of town.

She was so focused on the thrill of driving the Camaro that she'd missed the hushed conversation Caleb had on his cell. He hung up just as she sped toward a waiting police car on the side of the road.

"Slow down, Alex. You don't want a ticket."

"It's just J.T." To prove her point, she rolled down the window and waved as she passed him.

Caleb's face paled as though he expected the lights and sirens to be on their tails any second now, but instead her phone rang. She pressed the accept button without even checking to see who was calling. "Hey, J.T."

"Please say that was you driving that Camaro."

"Nice, huh?"

"Damn straight. I'll let you off the hook this time because that is such a sweet ride, but you'd better slow down before you get to Moffit's Crossroads. There's a super trooper waiting there."

"Thanks for the heads up." She eased up on the accelerator. "Talk to you later."

"Yeah, you'd better. I want to know what driving that machine was like." J.T. hung up with a laugh.

She turned to Caleb. "See? Nothing to worry about."

"Point taken. Once again, you've proven you know this town." He settled back in his seat and set his phone on his

114

lap. "Enjoying it?"

"Too much. There's no chance you'd be willing to sell me this baby, is there?"

"Not as long as I'm breathing."

She slowed down to the speed limit as she approached the area J.T. had warned her about. "So, what happened in the kitchen?"

"I got most of my questions answered."

Her insides knotted. "And?"

"And I think you deserve a night away from the drama so we can just be ourselves."

"We had a chance to be ourselves at Bubba's last night."

He closed his eyes, and a hint of a smile played on his lips. "Just drive."

"So you're not going to tell me what Kourtney said?"

"Maybe, but first, I need to make sense of it all. Besides, I told her I'd leave town if she answered my questions, and I figured my wingman could come with me."

"And what's the plan?"

His smile widened, but his eyes still remained closed. "I'll let you know in a bit. By the way, after seeing the way you handle this car, I've finally come up with a call sign for you."

"What?"

"'Hot Wheels.'"

She laughed and merged onto the interstate, heading toward Atlanta.

They were about twenty miles into Georgia when his phone rang. This time, she hung on every word of his conversation.

"What do you have for me?" he asked and nodded a few times before adding, "The Four Seasons, huh? Nice." A few more sounds of agreement followed. "And dinner at STK? Wow, you've outdone yourself, Frank."

Her mind started filling in the blanks. Caleb's brother, Frank, was a linebacker for the Atlanta Wildcats. That must be who he was talking to, but it didn't explain the mention of the hotel or the restaurant.

"Thanks again," Caleb continued. "I'm looking forward to tonight." He hung up the phone with a huge grin.

"Care to tell me what your plan is now?"

"I'm taking you out for a night on the town."

She squirmed in her seat. This was sounding like more than just a night on the town. "Like a thank-you gift or something?"

His grin faded, and his eyes darkened with the same desire she'd witnessed last night. "Maybe. Maybe not. It just depends on where things go."

Her nipples hardened. If she had her way, they'd be heading straight to the hotel room and not leaving until morning. "You don't have to go all out to impress me, Caleb. You've seen how I like to spend my evenings. I'm just a simple country girl."

He chuckled. "There's nothing simple about you. And please, just humor me. I want to treat you to something nice."

"Why?"

"Because you deserve nice things, Alex, and don't let anyone make you believe you don't."

"I never have. Besides, this is my idea of nice things—

driving a classic car, getting away from my sister's wedding madness…" *Spending time with you.*

"Are you saying you want to turn back?"

She shook her head. "I'm just letting you know that unlike Kourtney, you don't have to drop a few grand to impress me."

"I know." He closed his eyes again. "But since you saved me a few hundred bucks on the B&B—"

"Miss Martha told you about that, huh?"

"She mentioned you two had worked out a deal. You didn't have to do that, you know."

"I know, but she was putting you up for a few nights at the last minute and couldn't afford the entire repair bill for her car, so it just worked out that way." She glanced down at her worn jeans. "And in truth, I'm a little worried I may be underdressed for a night on the town."

He cracked open one eye and looked her over. "You'll have time to go shopping. I'll give you some cash when we get into town."

She groaned and bit back to the urge to tell him what she really wanted. "I'm going to have to get a dress, aren't I?"

His grin returned. "I didn't say that. In fact, you looked pretty good this afternoon wearing nothing at all."

Her cheeks grew warm. "I doubt they'll let me parade around Midtown like Lady Godiva."

"Too bad." He shifted in his seat. "On second thought, that's probably a good thing. I'd have to fight off too many horny guys."

She rolled her eyes and laughed. "And if I don't find anything I like and end up dining like this?"

"Then I'm okay with that, so long as I get to eat a nice dinner with you."

The pitter-patter of her heart quickened, and her hope returned. Maybe this was his way of showing her that he was over her sister and wanted her. "And at the hotel?"

That sexy grin returned. "Dinner first."

And if she was lucky, dessert would totally make up for having to dress up for dinner.

CHAPTER NINE

Caleb reached into his pocket and rubbed his lucky charm just before entering the crowded lobby of STK, one of the elite steakhouses in Atlanta. He scanned the room for Alex, but when he didn't see her, he made his way to the hostess stand and gave his name.

"Your party's already here," she said with a smile, and some of the tension eased from his shoulders.

When he'd dropped Alex off at Lenox Square, he'd half expected her to bolt, especially since he knew she hated dressing up. Part of him felt bad about taking her to a place where she couldn't wear her jeans, but Frank had made the reservation, not him.

He followed the hostess upstairs to the quieter dining room and searched for Alex. But the table she led him to had an entirely different redhead waiting for him.

Frank.

"Caleb!" His brother jumped from his chair and wrapped Caleb in a massive bear hug, which was easy enough for Frank to do. He had a good four inches of height and seventy pounds of muscle on him, perfect for knocking quarterbacks to the turf during football season. "It's good to see you back in one piece." He paused and gave him a teasing grin. "You are in one piece, right?"

"Yeah, pretty sure I am." Although his heart was a total wreck now. "What are you doing here?"

"What do you think I'm doing? Having dinner with my big brother."

"That's nice and all, but I think I hinted that I wanted to take a girl out for a nice dinner."

"Are you saying she won't have a good time with me? Maybe we can share her, eh?" he continued to tease with a playful nudge.

"No, Frank, I was serious." He slid into the booth, wondering what else could go wrong tonight. "I wanted to have some time alone with Alex." *And find out if she was the one behind those emails, because if she was...*

He gulped. Could it really be as simple as that? Could he have been in love with her all this time and never realized it?

Frank stared past him, his jaw going slack. "And I can see why."

Caleb turned around and had to do a double take at the woman standing in front of him. Alex had always been cute, but now she was absolutely stunning. A sparkling clip pulled her auburn hair out of her face and allowed it to tumble down around her shoulders. A strapless silver dress enhanced her modest curves and ended just below her ass. That, combined with high heels the same metallic shade, made her shapely legs seem to go on forever.

He stood up, unable to take his eyes off her. "You look nice, Alex. Real nice."

A smile brightened her face far more than the modest makeup she'd put on. "Thanks, Caleb." She shoved a wad of bills into his hand. "Here's your change from my shopping trip."

Frank chose that moment to interrupt. "Hi, I'm Frank, Caleb's much handsomer and very available younger brother." He took her hand and placed a kiss on it. "And who are you, lovely lady?"

She turned to Caleb with an arched brow. "Is he always this full of shit?"

Her quip instantly lifted his mood and made him forget about his disappointment. "Sometimes he's worse." He wrapped his arm around her waist and placed a kiss on her temple, inhaling the seductive perfume she'd worn tonight. "Sorry, bro, but she's with me."

"There's still a chance I can change her mind." Frank retreated back to his seat. "She's definitely a step up from your last girlfriend."

Alex pressed her twitching lips together, laughter dancing in her whiskey colored eyes, but all Caleb wanted to do was smack his brother.

She slid into the booth next to him and immediately started talking football with Frank. Any worries he had about the evening vanished. The conversation was as seamless as it had been last night with her friends. No snobbery. No awkwardness. It was like she'd always been part of the family.

And so very different than her sister, who'd barely managed to hold a civil conversation with any member of his family.

As dinner went on, the discussion turned to classic cars, and Alex started describing the updates she was making to her Roadrunner. "I'm working on deactivating some of the cylinders so when I don't need that much power, I can save gas."

Frank's brows furrowed. "Sounds complicated."

"It's not that bad. At least I'm getting to use my degree some."

The muscles between Caleb's shoulders tightened. "I didn't know you had a college degree."

"Yeah, in mechanical engineering." She waved him off as though it were nothing. "But I'm still running into some trouble getting the timing right for when I need that extra boost of power."

She continued gabbing on about the tweaks she was making to the engine, but he drifted away from what she was saying. Alex was far smarter than most people gave her credit for, including him. All this time, he'd dismissed her as just a simple mechanic. But an engineer? What other surprises was she hiding?

One thing became clear, however. If she was smart enough to earn a degree in engineering, she was more than likely able to hack into Kourtney's account. The question was, why?

Frank looked more and more lost as Alex continued, and it wasn't long before he interrupted. "Excuse me, but I see a friend over there that I want to say hello to." He left the table and disappeared down the stairs to the lounge below.

A flush rose into Alex's cheeks. "I guess I got a little carried away."

"Don't apologize. Frank was always the dimmest out of all of us." Caleb brushed a stray lock of her hair that had fallen free from the clip. "You, on the other hand, never cease to amaze me."

Her grin returned, and she dropped her voice to a seductive purr as she leaned closer. "Maybe there are a few more ways I can amaze you."

The blood shot straight to his groin. "I certainly bet there are."

"Perhaps we should go back to the hotel and find out." She nipped his bottom lip, intensifying the ache in his cock.

"Careful—I think Atlanta has the same public lewdness laws as Jackson Grove."

"Why do you think I suggested the hotel room?"

"But it would be rude to bail on my brother," he reminded her just before she silenced him with a kiss.

After the way last night ended, he'd expected some hesitation, some restraint from her. Instead, she immersed him in the same passion she did before. Alex never did anything half-heartedly, including seducing him. Not that she had to try hard. The more he learned about her, the deeper he fell.

She pulled away, her eyes contented and heavy as though she'd just come in his bed instead of merely sharing a smoldering kiss. "Thank you."

"For what?"

"For being amazed by me."

A new ache surfaced in his chest, making him forget about the one in his pants. How many others were just like him, so blinded by the superficial dazzle of Kourtney that they failed to see the true gem hiding in her shadow?

He traced the rim of her mouth with his thumb, committing the curve of her lips to his memory. "So I'm forgiven?"

Her eyes widen, and she drew in a sharp breath. "What did you do?"

"I made a fool of myself over the wrong woman, and it took a good wingman to show me what I was truly missing."

"That's what a good wingman does—point out what you're missing."

"And yet I have the feeling you still have more to show me, Hot Wheels."

"Maybe so." She licked her lips and turned her attention to her almost empty plate. "Caleb, did—"

"Sorry I ran off like that," Frank interrupted, and Caleb bit back a groan of frustration.

He'd been so close to finding out the truth. But it didn't matter. He was already ninety-nine percent certain Alex had written those letters. The how and why could wait a bit longer.

His brother sat down and carved another chunk off his medium rare porterhouse. "I saw one of my teammates over there, and we made plans to meet up at The Cheetah Club later tonight. Want to join us?"

This time, Caleb couldn't hold back the groan. "Promise me you'll stay out of trouble, Frank."

"Who says I'm going to get into any trouble?"

Alex inched toward the edge of the booth. "Maybe this is my cue to go visit the ladies' room." She gave his hand a little squeeze before leaving.

"Damn, she is a hot piece of ass, Caleb." Frank stabbed his fork into his steak, but his eyes were glued on Alex as she walked away.

Caleb curled his still-warm hand into a fist. "Don't talk

about her like that."

"I meant it as a compliment. What's a girl like that doing with you, anyway?"

"I'm her date for a wedding."

"Right, and I'm going to enter the priesthood." Frank studied him while he finished chewing. "How serious is it?"

He thought about the ring he'd gotten for Kourtney and imagined it on Alex's finger instead. "Serious enough."

Frank shook his head like he thought Caleb had lost his mind. "You're forgiven for having such thoughts, since she seems like she'd be an awesome fuck."

"I wouldn't know."

The knife and fork fell from Frank's hands. "Who are you, and what have you done with my brother? Seriously, you're pulling my leg, right? Please tell me you've gotten her in the sack."

"No, I haven't slept with her." *Yet.* But if their earlier conversation was any indication, he was in for one helluva good time when they got back to the room.

"Did you turn gay over there in Afghanistan?"

Caleb squirmed in his seat. "No."

"Then why haven't you banged her? It's quite obvious she's open to the idea, and you've never been one to turn down an invitation. Hell, you were the ones slipping us condoms when we were younger and telling us never to miss out on a great fuck."

Her comment from last night echoed through his mind, and a wave of shame cooled the remnants of his desire. *If this is going to happen between us, then I need to know it's because I'm something more to you than just a quick fuck.* The old Caleb would've said a few tried and true phrases to reassure her so he could've gotten what he wanted. But last night, he'd said nothing. He hadn't wanted to trick Alex, even though he knew then she was more than just a quick lay. But now that he knew without a doubt his relationship with Kourtney was over, he was finally free to give himself to Alex.

"Let's just say this one is different."

"If I catch you holding her purse and her Chihuahua, I'm going to disown you."

Caleb laughed, and the tension eased. "I don't think I'll ever be in danger of that with Alex. It would be more like me holding her socket wrench and minding her Rottweiler."

"Seriously, if things don't pan out with you, give her my number." Frank threw down his napkin and gave a charming grin to someone behind Caleb. "That was quick."

Alex shrugged and slid back into the booth. "I'm not much of a primper."

Even though it was quite obvious she'd applied a fresh coat of gloss that made her lips look more tempting than ever. Caleb slid his arm around her and pulled her close, savoring the warmth of her bare skin and imagining what it would feel like when she was lying naked beneath him.

"My brother was just telling me that he's your date for a wedding."

She looked up at Frank, her brown eyes sparkling in the dim lights of the restaurant, and turned up her Southern drawl. "Yes, it was very kind of him to rescue a damsel in distress like little ol' me."

Caleb nearly choked. "I doubt anyone would ever consider you a damsel in need of rescuing."

"Maybe you can return the favor." Frank's voice hinted at mischief, and Caleb fought back a groan. "Caleb is in need of a date for our brother's wedding next month."

He opened his mouth to say no, but his tongue refused to move. The more he thought about it, the more he liked the idea of bringing Alex home to meet his family. "One battle at a time."

"Agreed," she added. "Let's see how Caleb feels after surviving the insanity this weekend."

At least she didn't say no.

"If you need a reference, let me know. Caleb taught me everything I know."

Caleb fought back another groan. Was Frank purposely trying to sabotage his chances with Alex?

His brother rose from the table like a lumbering giant. "Time for me to take off. If you want to hang out at The Cheetah Club later tonight, you know where to find me."

"Stay out of trouble, Frank. I'm not bailing you out of jail this time."

Frank laid his hand over his heart. "Is that anything to say to your little brother?" He winked and disappeared into the crowded lounge below.

"That was nice of him to leave just before we get the bill," Alex murmured, the corner of her mouth rising into a wry smile.

"That's Frank for you." Caleb pulled out his wallet and flagged down their server. "It's fine—I can cover it."

But when the check arrived, there were two surprises

waiting for him inside the check holder. The first was a credit card receipt bearing Frank's autograph. The second was a wrapped condom with a note attached to it.

It's time I returned the favor, Big Bro.

The tips of Caleb's ears burned, and he snapped the holder closed. But it was too late, judging by the single cocked brow Alex gave him.

She opened it back up and retrieved the condom. "Planning on getting lucky tonight, flyboy?"

"Just a private joke." He tried to snatch the condom back, but she kept it out of his reach. "I apologize if it offended you."

"Do I look offended?" She leaned in and whispered in his ear, "The only thing that would offend me is if we *don't* use this tonight."

His mind clouded with desire, but he remained grounded enough to remember what she'd said last night. "Just so you know, this will definitely be more than just a quick fuck."

"I certainly hope so."

The last of his hesitations vanished. Going home with her seemed as natural as breathing. "Then let's not waste any more time."

He followed her out of the booth and down the stairs, catching her as she wobbled in her high heels.

"Damn it, I hate these things," she muttered as she regained her balance.

"You have no idea how sexy you look in them."

"Then I suppose the torture of trying to walk in them is worth it."

"Want me to carry you back to the hotel?"

She pressed her body against him, revving up the blood flow to his groin. "The idea has merit."

But when they go outside, he spied a taxi dropping someone off. "I have a better idea."

He snagged the taxi and helped Alex into it. "The Four Seasons."

"That's just around the block," the driver said.

His hand grazed her bare legs, and another idea entered his mind. "Then take the long way around," he replied just before he pulled her into a kiss that made him forget about everything else.

Alex responded with the same fire she had before, but with every second that passed, the passion intensified. She closed the space between them, their bodies glued together in a tangle of arms and legs. He tasted the sweetness of the wine from dinner on her tongue, inhaled the exotic scent of her perfume, ran his hand up her silky thighs until he reached the lacy triangle of fabric that covered her pussy. He pressed his palm against it, his fingers pushing past her underwear to dive into her warm heat. The soft moan that rose from her throat nearly sent him over the edge. Dear God, he'd never wanted a woman so badly.

He came up for air and realized the taxi was pulling into the hotel. "I thought I said to take the long way."

"I did." The driver smirked into his rearview mirror. "You two can keep going back there, but the meter's still running."

Alex grabbed Caleb by the lapels of his jacket. "This might be more fun without an audience."

"You're going to have to walk in front of me as we go

through the lobby." He pointed to the obvious bulge under his zipper.

She exited the taxi with a laugh while he fished out a few bills for the fare, ignoring the envious expression the driver gave him. He never worried for a second that she'd flirt with another man like her sister had. Alex was all his tonight, and he was determined to show her how much she meant to him.

When he got out, she took him by the hand and wrapped it around her waist so he could hold her close in front of him as they crossed the lobby to the elevators. Each step was its own form of agony with her ass rubbing against his aching cock.

As soon as the elevator doors closed behind them, Alex turned around and gave him another searing kiss that made him want to hit the emergency stop button so he could finish without interruption. A ding ended the kiss abruptly, and Alex managed to move in front of him just as an older couple entered the elevator and turned to face the doors.

"What floor are we on, anyway?"

"Eighteen." He nuzzled the side of her neck, pressing his lips to the place where her rapid pulse throbbed.

"We would be near the top."

"Don't blame me. Frank made the reservation."

The other couple got off at the fifteenth floor, but Alex didn't pick up where they had left off. Instead, her movements became more reserved, and his heart sank. She was having second thoughts.

They walked down the hallway in silence, the sudden tension making him feel like there was a wide gulf between them instead of a few inches. He pulled out his key card and hesitated. "Alex, if you don't want to do this…"

"I want this." She guided the card into the slot. "I've wanted you since the moment I met you."

"Good, because when I'm with you, I feel like I'm home."

He never imagined such a simple confession would make her glow like it did. The brightness of her smile chased away the lingering shadows in his heart and bathed him in its light. It had the same effect on him the emails had—bolstering his spirits and injecting him with a love that was more precious than anything money could buy.

He held the door open for her. "I have just one request."

"What's that?" She turned to him and threaded her fingers through his hair.

"Leave the shoes on."

She pulled him closer, her grin widening. "Fine, but I get to be on top."

"I can live with that." He covered her mouth with his own and blindly searched for her zipper as her tongue danced with his.

Her dress was the first article of clothing that was shed, quickly followed by his jacket and shirt. By the time they'd crossed the room to the bed, she was in the process of shimmying her panties off while he unfastened her bra. He'd just freed the final hook when she pushed him back on the mattress, giving him his first glance at her in all her naked glory. He'd never seen a more beautiful woman, and he couldn't believe she was here with him.

She crawled on top of him, her skin flushed with

desire, her brown eyes as hungry as her kisses. "What did you do with that condom?"

"It's next to my lucky charm."

She retrieved it from his pants and wasted no time removing his shorts and rolling it on. "I need you now."

"Then let's not waste any more time."

She straddled his lap, still wearing those silver high heels, and positioned her opening over the tip of his cock. Inch by inch, she took him in until he was fully sheathed inside her tight walls.

He inhaled through his teeth. "My God, you feel so good."

"I'm only getting started." She rolled her hips, creating a subtle friction that sent jolts along the length of his shaft. "That's better."

"Please, Alex, if you don't start moving soon, I'm going to lose my mind."

"Patience, flyboy."

But she lifted her hips, rising until just his tip was inside her, before sliding back down. She repeated her actions, each time faster until they found the perfect rhythm. He watched her with awe. She was like a goddess riding him. She threw her head back, the arch of her neck practically begging his lips to touch her there. A purr of contentment rose from her throat when he placed a kiss there.

Caleb pressed his palm into the small of her back, changing the angle of penetration. Her breath caught, and she dug her fingers into his shoulders. "Yes, there. Right there."

The rocking of her pelvis quickened and grew erratic. He tried to calm her movements, to guide her hips with

132

his hands, but she would have none of it. She fought him, lost in her own ecstasy, and captured his lips once more. He tasted the desperation, her need, in her kiss. She was close, so very close.

But so was he. It had been wildly erotic watching her ride him with her silver heels on, never mind how wonderful it felt to be inside her. But when he looked into her eyes, he saw more than just sexual lust. He saw peace, acceptance, wonder, and warmth. His chest tightened when he realized whatever was developing between them went beyond the physical. Alex was in love with him. And somewhere along the way, he'd fallen just as hard for her.

Her inner walls clenched his cock, and his name fell from her lips. A shudder signaling her release wracked her body and flowed into him, triggering his own. Pure bliss rushed through him like a 6 g nosedive and blurred his vision. He came, crying her name and wrapping his arms around her like she was the only thing that could save him from a complete G-LOC.

But when his vision cleared, she was still there, her forehead pressed against his. A choked laugh alternated with a sound that bordered on a sob in every rapid breath she exhaled.

He brushed her hair back to find a hesitant smile twitching on her full lips. "You okay?"

She nodded. "You?"

"Yeah." He eased back on the mattress, taking her with him and holding her close. "I'd say I'm feeling pretty damn good right now."

"Me, too." She chewed her bottom lip a moment before adding, "Do you think we can do that again?"

He opened the nightstand drawer and pulled out the box of condoms he'd bought earlier.

Alex raised a brow. "That certain you were going to get laid tonight, huh?"

"Aren't you glad I was prepared for the best-case scenario?"

She gave him a soft, sexy laugh that revived the blood flow to his cock. "Just let me know when you're ready to go."

"Most definitely." He pulled her closer, feeling the steady drum of her heart through her chest, and grinned. No matter what happened after tonight, he knew life would never be dull with Alex.

CHAPTER TEN

Alex opened her eyes and zeroed in on the thin rim of sunlight that poured through a crack in the drapes and sliced across the bed. It was morning. The pleasant ache between her thighs reminded her of the previous night's activities. She'd lost count how many times she'd come with Caleb inside her, discovering how wonderful he felt as they tried out position after position, all with her still wearing those ridiculous heels. But when they'd both reached the point of sheer exhaustion, he'd removed her shoes and cradled her in his arms until she'd fallen asleep.

She'd known sex would be great with Caleb, but she'd never imagined how well they fit together. Hours had passed, but neither one of them had moved. His warm body encircled hers like he'd been made for her. Their hands remained entwined, and their chests rose and fell with each breath in sync like a perfectly balanced engine.

Watch it, girl—you're all ready to give him your heart, and you don't even know for sure if he's over your sister.

But she wasn't going to ruin the moment by waking him up and asking about his conversation with Kourtney. If his behavior was any indication, that conversation yesterday afternoon had been the final nail in the coffin of his dead relationship.

Her cell phone's ring tone for the shop shattered the silence and sent her heart into overdrive. She tried to rise, but Caleb pinned her to the mattress. "It can wait," he said in a sleepy voice.

"No, it can't." She wrestled free from him, wondering what had happened to cause Jermaine to call her from her office line. The constant ringing guided her to where she'd stowed her phone in the shopping bag that held the clothes she'd worn yesterday. She grabbed it and hit the answer button. "What's wrong?"

"Where the hell are you?" Kourtney replied, her voice dripping with anger.

Her blood ran cold. "What are you doing at the garage?"

"I'm standing here in this filthy, God-awful place because you were supposed to meet me out front half an hour ago. And when you didn't answer the door or my calls, I was forced to use this phone."

Alex pressed her palm to her pounding temple and sank into a nearby chair. She'd set her phone to the do-not-disturb settings last night. The only calls that would get through would be ones from the shop. "Remind me what was on the agenda today."

"We're supposed to be at the dress shop in Buckhead in less than two hours for our final fittings." A few muttered cuss words followed. "I knew you would find a way to ruin my wedding. You always ruin everything."

"Relax, Kourtney. I'm already in Atlanta."

A pause filled the line as though her sister was filling in the missing pieces. "What are you doing in Atlanta?"

"Caleb and I had dinner with his brother and ended up

staying the night." *And having wild sex until the wee hours of the morning.*

Upon hearing his name, Caleb lifted his head and propped himself up on his elbow, giving her a come-hither stare that tempted her to end the call right then and hop back into bed.

"I would've appreciated that information, you know, instead of wasting half an hour here." The sound of high heels clicking along the cement punctuated each syllable of her sister's words. "I'm on my way right now, and don't you dare show up late to the dress shop."

A click ended the call, and Alex threw her phone back into the bag. Leave it to her sister to ruin a perfect morning.

"What was that about?" Caleb asked, still lying naked in the bed.

"I forgot I was supposed to meet her for our final dress fittings today." She ran her fingers through her hair, hitting each tangled snarl along the way. Last night had been fun, but the guilt of her sister's words weighed upon her. *You always ruin everything.* That pretty much summed up her relationship with her mom and sister. No matter what she did, she'd never be more than a disappointment to them. "I need to start getting ready so I won't be late."

She stepped into the shower and turned the hot water on, letting the steam numb her mind. A blast of cold jerked her back to reality, and she turned to find Caleb had joined her.

"You forgot the shampoo," he said, holding up the mini-bottle provided by the hotel.

"Don't forget the conditioner." It was the only hope

she had of untangling her crazy hair.

He held up the other mini-bottle in the other hand. "I didn't." She tried to take it from him, but he held it out of reach. "Let me."

At first, she wanted to tell him she was perfectly capable of washing her own hair, but the minute his fingers started massaging her scalp, she surrendered. "This is nice."

"I thought you could use a little special treatment after that phone call."

"It's just Kourtney. She's always finding some fault with me."

"Don't let her get to you, Alex." He guided her back under the spray of water and rinsed the shampoo out. "I've come to the conclusion that she thinks no one is perfect except for her."

"What else have you come to the conclusion of regarding her?"

He finished working the conditioner through her hair before replying. "That it was over between us long before I deployed, and I was too stupid to see it." He tilted her chin around to him. "In fact, I've been too stupid to see a lot of things lately, but I'm learning."

Her stomach tightened, and she licked her lips. Is this where he called her out over the emails? "And what else have you seen?"

"You." He stared into her eyes for several breaths before sweeping his gaze over her body. "I'm sorry I was too blind to see you before, Alex, but now that I have..."

Her chest ached, but she couldn't tell if it was fear or hope. "And?"

"And now I never want to let you go." He pulled her to him and kissed her in a way that made her toes curl and drew the very air from her lungs. "Let me show you," he murmured after he ended the kiss.

He grabbed the soap and ran it along the flat of her stomach. His fingers followed, gliding up to her breasts and cupping them in his hands under the water. "You're so beautiful."

He bent down and captured one nipple between his teeth. A shock of pleasure shot straight down to the pit of her stomach.

"You never cease to amaze me," he continued when he was finished with her breasts. His hands continued lower to the already sensitive junction of her thighs, the hard ridge of his erection pressed against her hip. "And I look forward to being even more amazed by you."

His thumb grazed her clit. A whimper rose from her throat, and she melted into his arms as his fingers swirled around the aching nub of flesh. Faster, harder, tighter until the tension mounting inside her exploded, and she forgot about everything but him.

In her post-orgasmic haze, she was vaguely aware of him rinsing the last of the citrus-scented conditioner from her hair and turning off the water. A fluffy towel wrapped around her just before he lifted her into his arms and carried her back to bed. The metallic crackle of a condom wrapper told her he hadn't finished making her come. A few seconds later, he hovered over her, cradling her face between his hands.

She looked up in his blue eyes and found the one thing she'd always dreamed she would see shining from them.

Love.

"I think you're perfect just the way you are, Alex."

He slid into her, and she finally understood what he'd said last night about feeling like he was home. She was home in his arms, lying under him as he moved inside her with tender slowness. Last night had been wild, passionate sex, but it paled in comparison to now. This time, he was making love to her and silently begging her to give more than just her body to him. He wanted all of her, found perfection in her flaws, and made her feel whole. How could she *not* fall in love with him?

She stared into his eyes as he brought her to her climax and sent her over the edge. The only word spoken between them was her name just before he came. And in the minutes that followed, she finally whispered, "I think you're perfect, too."

****

Alex blew out a breath of frustration as Caleb pulled into the parking lot of the bridal boutique. Kourtney's BMW was already there, which meant Alex had a shit storm waiting for her inside. But she would gladly suffer through hours of her sister's rants in exchange for the moments she'd spent in Caleb's arms this morning.

"Should I hang around?" he asked.

She shook her head. Kourtney was already going to be pissed enough that she was late. She didn't need to bring Caleb into this. "I'll be fine."

"I don't mind waiting."

"I know you don't, but I want to spare you the drama." She pulled the key to her place off the ring. "Just make yourself at home, and I'll be there in a few hours if

Kourtney doesn't kill me first."

He gave her a crooked smile like he thought she was crazy, but took the key. "Call if you need me to rescue you sooner."

"I will." She opened the door, but he grabbed her by the hand and pulled her into one more searing kiss that made her hate every article of clothing she wore. "What was that for?"

"To give you something to remember when she's trying to get under your skin." He gave her a sexy grin that told her he'd probably be picking up a new box of condoms on the way home. "By the way, can I use your computer to check my email?"

"Sure. The password is "IROC Z28," all caps with an underscore between the words."

He laughed. "Why am I not surprised?" He placed a chaste kiss on her cheek. "See you in a few hours."

The warm glow that had surrounded her all morning lingered even after he drove away. Her plan had worked. Caleb had finally fallen in love with her, but there was only one thing that kept her from celebrating. She still hadn't told him about the letters.

Tonight, she promised herself. She would come clean about the emails tonight, and hopefully, he wouldn't mind her deception once he learned the reason behind them.

Kourtney and the other bridesmaids were still waiting in the front of the boutique when she entered, but that didn't stop Bridezilla from singling Alex out. "You're late."

"By what? A minute? Besides, it's not like they've pulled out the dresses yet."

Mindy placed a hand on Kourtney's shoulder and pulled her back, whispering something in her ear. Whatever she said, it calmed Alex's sister down enough to where she could give a halfway genuine smile when the staff appeared from the back room with a rack of dresses.

The actual fitting was easy enough. Alex lacked the artificial curves of some of the other women in the bridal party, and her dress had fit well even without alterations. She quickly changed back into her clothes and waited for her sister to finish.

She had to hand it to her sister—she certainly knew how to make an entrance. Kourtney pulled back the curtain and emerged from the fitting room like a queen holding court. Her strapless white dress hugged her figure and cascaded to the floor in a long train fit for royalty. She put one hand on her hip and stuck out her chest. "How do I look?"

Her other bridesmaids gathered around her with *ooh*s and *ahh*s, but Alex stayed back. Knowing her luck, she'd step on the train and rip it two days before the wedding.

After she'd been inundated with compliments, Kourtney focused her attention on Alex. "Be a good little sister and help me out of the dress."

"Are you sure? I don't want to do anything to ruin your wedding."

Kourtney gave her a tight smile. "Just promise to be careful." She whirled around, whipping her skirts behind her, and disappeared behind the curtain.

Alex tiptoed into the dressing room in the same way Kourtney had always entered the garage, taking care not to touch anything. "Is there a reason why you asked me and not Mindy?"

"Yes." She stared at her reflection, both hands on her hips and waited. "Start with the top hook."

There had to be at least thirty tiny hook-and-eyes holding the dress together. Alex fumbled with the first one for about ten seconds before unfastening it. "I'm sorry I wasn't at the garage this morning."

"Do you think I brought you back here to fuss about that?" Kourtney met Alex's gaze in the mirror. "I saw Caleb dropped you off this morning."

"So?"

"So I'm going to give you a bit of sisterly advice—don't fall too hard for him, Alex. He'll only end up breaking your heart."

"You have a lot of nerve trying to tell me that, especially after what you did to him."

"And you have a lot of nerve chasing after him when you know deep down inside you have no future with him."

Alex tugged a bit harder at the hooks. This conversation had gone on long enough. "Who says we don't have a future together?"

Kourtney swatted her hands away and turned around. "Then answer this question. If he asked you to pack up everything, leave Jackson Grove, and follow him to Utah, would you be able to do it?"

Her mouth went dry, and a jab of fear paralyzed her.

"I thought as much." Kourtney turned back to the mirror and squared her shoulders. "Like it or not, you're just like me. Neither one of us is cut out to be an Air Force wife, and he won't give up flying. You're only kidding yourself if you think you have any chance of a happy ending with him."

Alex finished unfastening the final hooks in silence, mulling over her sister's words. She'd been so wrapped up in trying to make Caleb fall in love with her that she never even considered what would happen next. Caleb had to leave on Sunday to report back to his base, and she would remain back in Jackson Grove with her garage and the life she'd built there. The heavy dose of reality dropped into her stomach like a hemi engine. She couldn't imagine giving it all up to move across the country, nor could she imagine asking him to give up what he loved the most.

The sinking feeling in her gut intensified into nausea as she exited the dressing room. She refused to be like Kourtney and ask him to leave the Air Force for her, but in making that choice, she was grounding their relationship before it even had a chance to take off.

CHAPTER ELEVEN

Caleb unlocked Alex's computer and opened up a browser. Time to do some reconnaissance work. He was ninety-nine percent certain that Alex had written those emails, but until he had proof, he was going on nothing more than a hunch.

And he needed more than that, especially after he'd almost told her he loved her this morning. In the heat of the moment, when everything felt so right, it was easy to forget about all the unanswered questions. But he'd managed to keep it from slipping out.

He went to the home page for the web-based email service and started typing in Kourtney's email address. The auto fill popped up with the complete address, and his heart skipped a beat. Someone had used this computer to access that account, but it still didn't give him the proof he needed. He moved to the password section and held his breath while he entered Alex's password. The hourglass appeared and did a couple of rotations before taking him to another page.

Jackpot!

He went straight to an inbox that contained nothing but the emails he'd sent while he was deployed.

Caleb leaned back in the chair and stared at the list, his

145

mind flying at supersonic speeds. He seriously doubted Kourtney would've come to Alex's place to use her computer in the first place, and he knew she'd never use a classic muscle car as a password. Therefore, it was safe to conclude Alex had been the one to hack her sister's account and change the password. Also, if Kourtney was to be believed, this had happened shortly after he left for Afghanistan, making it easy to deduce that Alex—not Kourtney—had written the emails.

That left only one question. *Why?*

And that made his mind ache. Why had she hacked her sister's email? Why did she send those emails? Why did she sign them as Kourtney and not as herself? And why hadn't she come clean about them?

After finding no answers on his own, he pulled out his phone and scrolled through his contact list. He could ask Adam what he thought about this. Or maybe his mom. Or maybe even his twin, Dan. But every time his finger hovered over a number, he chickened out until he got to Gideon's number and found a solution.

His youngest brother answered on the first ring. "Hey, Caleb, how are you doing?"

"Well enough." He ran his finger along the neck of his shirt. "Is Sarah around?"

"Why?"

"Just put her on the phone if she's there. I need some feminine advice, and I know she won't give me any crap."

It had been a long shot expecting to reach her by calling Gideon, but his brother's assistant was never far away. The family often credited her from keeping Gid out of trouble in Hollywood, especially since she was more

146

than familiar with fame's dark side.

"Fine, I'll go get her, but when you're done, I'd at least like more than a few words from you."

A moment later, Sarah came on the line. "The Kid said you wanted to speak to me," she said, calling Gideon by the nickname she'd given him years ago.

"Yeah, I need some insight into the female psyche."

"And you decided to ask me?"

"You're a redhead, so maybe you'll have better insight into this woman since she's one, too."

"Oh, yeah, because all redheads are the same." Sarah's usual dry sarcasm filtered across the line. "What did she do?"

"She posed as her sister and sent me a bunch of emails while I was deployed."

"And?"

"And I kind of fell for her. But why would she do that? Why make me fall in love with her sister when she's really the one I should be falling for?"

"Ah, we have a classic Cyrano case here."

"Cyrano? Wasn't he the guy with the big nose?"

"Bingo. Glad to know those g-forces haven't squeezed all the intelligence from your brain."

"Not completely, but that still doesn't tell me why she did it."

"Cyrano—the guy with the big nose—was secretly in love with Roxane, but he didn't think he stood a chance, especially when he saw that this hot guy in his unit, Christian, was making a move on her. So, he offered to help Christian woo Roxane through a bunch of letters that he wrote under the hot guy's identity. Following me so far?"

Caleb got up from the chair and paced the loft apartment. "Yep, and it's starting to finally make sense. So what happened to Cyrano?"

"It's kind of a tragic ending. Roxane ends up marrying the pretty boy, and Cyrano dies never telling her that he was the author of the letters."

A chill coursed down his spine. So very close to what almost happened here. "Why would he keep that a secret?"

"Pride, self-doubt, frustration—you name it. So, is there a reason why this redhead would think she doesn't stand a chance with you?"

"Yeah, but I'm starting to see things much more clearly now."

"Good. Then don't be a ditz like Roxane and marry the wrong girl. Brains are always better than boobs."

A shuffle filled the line, and Gideon's voice returned. "Did that help?"

"Immensely, but why do I have the feeling Sarah's pissed off at you?"

"Long story, but I think she's a little perturbed with the model I'm dating."

"'Perturbed' doesn't begin to explain it," Sarah shouted in the background.

"Hold on a sec." Caleb could almost picture Gideon running from the room and his irate assistant. The crash of waves echoed in the distance when his brother spoke again. "Sorry, but Sarah can't stand Kinzy."

"Why?"

"It's like she said—she thinks brains are better than

boobs, and while Kinzy's smoking hot, I have to admit, there's not much up there."

"And why are you dating her again?"

"Would you turn down a chance to date a Victoria's Secret model?" The "wink-wink, nudge-nudge" tone in his voice told Caleb he'd done more than just go out on a few dates with her. "Besides, it's nothing serious. Just a bit of fun in between movies. And weren't you the one who told me to never turn down a chance to get laid?"

"I see I've been a bad influence on both you and Frank." Caleb rubbed his jaw. "Just make sure you don't knock her up."

"Not a chance. So, will we see you at Adam's wedding next month?"

"I'll be there."

"Good, because I missed out on seeing you the last time you were home, and we have some catching up to do."

"Will do. Stay out of trouble, and don't piss off Sarah."

"Nah, I'm not worried about Red," he said, using his own nickname for Sarah. "She huffs and puffs, but I know I can count on her. Later."

Caleb hung up his phone and retrieved his good luck charm. As he stared at the crooked halo, he flashed back to something Alex had said last night.

I've always wanted you.

Could she have felt this way about him before he deployed? Was she like Cyrano, constantly showing him what was in her heart only to have him not notice it?

He squeezed the figurine in his hand. He wouldn't be like Roxane.

149

****

It was late afternoon before Alex returned. She breezed into the loft with a garment bag in tow and collapsed on the couch. "I'll be so glad when this wedding is over."

Caleb glanced over his shoulder at the computer. He'd spent most of the day re-reading the letters, only this time hearing Alex speak the words instead of Kourtney. With each line, it became more and more clear that Alex had spoken from her heart. And with every letter, he fell deeper in love with her.

Now came the hard part. He sat next to her and looked her in the eye. "I know you wrote those emails."

Her face blanched, making her freckles stand out even more. Terror filled her eyes. Her mouth fell open, but no sound came out.

It was all the confirmation he needed. "Why?"

She turned away, crossing her arms around her chest in a self-hug. "Caleb, I…"

"I fell in love with the woman who wrote those letters, and I think I deserve to know why you deceived me."

She snapped her gaze back to him. "You fell in love with me?"

"Damn it, Alex, is this some game to you?" He bolted from the couch and ran his fingers through his hair. Could he have been as wrong about her as he had been about her sister? Were they both cut from the same fabric?

Alex caught his hand and placed over the spot where her heart beat. The steady rhythm soothed his rattled confidence.

"Will you please give me a chance to explain?"

"I'm listening."

150

She squeezed her eyes shut and drew in a deep breath. When she opened them again, the terror was gone, leaving only a silent plea for forgiveness. "I never set out to hurt you, Caleb. I was just so appalled by what Kourtney did that I wanted to spare you any pain while you were deployed. At first, it was simple enough to send a few emails to keep your spirits up and continue the illusion that you'd have someone waiting for you when you came home. I never intended for things to go where they did." She closed the space between them, keeping his hand over her heart. "I never tried to make you fall in love with me, but I'm not sorry you did."

He swallowed and tried to digest her confession. He wanted to believe her, but there were still too many unanswered questions. "You could've told me Sunday night."

"Would you have believed me?" When he didn't answer, she continued, "I knew you were still under Kourtney's spell. And when I saw that you were finally starting to notice me, well, I…" She released his hand and turned away. "You were the one who said there was something wrong about lying to make someone fall in love with you."

He reached into his pocket and squeezed his good luck charm. *How did things get so complicated? Do I even know what I want?*

Alex seemed to grow farther and farther away as the seconds ticked by, even though she hadn't moved an inch. If he didn't say something soon, he risked losing her altogether. And he couldn't bear that, not when he'd just discovered how wonderful she could be.

He guided her chin back toward him and waited for her to look at him. "I need to know the truth, Alex. All of it."

"Where do you want me to start? With the fact I've always had a thing for you and that you've never noticed me? With the fact that I should've stopped those letters months ago, but was I was too selfish to because I'd fallen in love with you? Or the fact that I'd only agreed to be your wingman this week in the hopes that maybe, just maybe, you would see me for me and forget about my sister?"

Tears glistened in her eyes, but she didn't stop. "I know what I did was wrong, Caleb. I know I shouldn't have played with your heart and deceived you, but I'm not lying when I tell you that I do love you, and I want you to be happy with whatever you decide, even if it means letting you go."

Now it was his turn to be left speechless. His chest tightened from the influx of emotion, tearing away the last shreds of doubt. This was what he needed to hear. This was what needed to know. And now, there was nothing holding him back.

He pulled her into his arms. "Damn it, Alex," he said just before kissing her.

She stiffened at first, but in a matter of seconds, she was kissing him back in the same unrestrained manner. The last walls keeping them apart tumbled down. Here was his home, the place where he was safe and loved, and he was going to do everything in his power to keep her.

She guided him toward her bedroom, never breaking their kiss. He tasted her love, her passion, her need with every flick of her tongue. He slipped his hands under her

152

T-shirt, running his fingers along the soft skin of her back and waiting for the moment when he could help her shed the clothing between them.

They bumped into the mattress, and he was finally forced to gulp in a few breaths. Alex took the opportunity to whip off her shirt and jeans before helping him do the same. They fell into bed locked in each other's arms, skin to skin, lips to lips. An ache formed at the base of his cock, intensifying with every roll of her hips beneath him.

"Where's a condom?" he asked, his voice tight with desperation.

She blindly reached into her nightstand drawer and pulled one out. "Here."

He slipped it on and positioned his cock. But instead of plunging inside like his body begged him to do, he paused and stared at the woman under him. There was no mistaking the love shining from her eyes as she looked up at him. A sense of wonder and contentment filled him. Out of all the men in the world, she wanted him. "I do see you, Alex."

She stroked her fingers along his jaw, her smile widening. "I know that now."

He slid into her and knew he'd found the only woman he'd need. Here in her arms, he was home.

CHAPTER TWELVE

A harsh buzzing of an alarm pulled Caleb from the most blissful sleep of his life. Alex stirred beside him. He tightened his arms around her. "Five more minutes."

She gave him a soft laugh and smacked the snooze button. "Easy for you to say. You're not the one who has to open up the shop in half an hour."

"Jermaine can open the shop." He rolled on top of her and pinned her hands above her head. Arousal stirred in his blood and sent it straight to his cock. "How about you call in sick so we can stay in bed all day?"

A hum of contentment rose from her throat as she closed her eyes and appeared to ponder his offer, but in the end, she shook her head. "Sorry, but I played hooky yesterday, and the cars won't fix themselves. Besides, I'll have to leave early to get cleaned up for the rehearsal dinner."

"And I suppose you'll need a date for that."

"If you want to tag along. I heard the McClures are doing some outdoors luau thing at their house." She bit her bottom lip, and a mischievous glow warmed her brown eyes. "Besides, I promise you I'll make it entertaining, maybe with a little horizontal hula later."

"That still doesn't take care of now." He shifted so his

growing erection pressed into her lower stomach.

"You are completely insatiable."

"Only when it comes to you." He tried to coax her into lingering in bed with another kiss, but her alarm blared to life again.

"Sorry, flyboy, but it's time for this working girl to get up." She placed a quick peck on his cheek. "Later."

He shifted to the side to let her get up, already missing the warmth of her body next to his. Was it possible to become addicted to someone after only two nights?

The sound of a shower came from the bathroom, and Alex came out a few minutes later with damp hair and glowing skin. She grabbed a pair of coveralls from the closet. "I'll start some coffee in the kitchen while you get dressed."

"I'm still too exhausted to move."

"Then I'm going to start questioning your stamina," she teased. "I thought pilots were supposed to be endurance athletes."

"Maybe you should come back to bed and continue my training."

"Love to, but can't. There's a busted fuel injector downstairs with my name on it."

"Ouch!" He threw his arm over his eyes. "I'm getting dumped for a fuel injector."

She gave him a playful swat with her towel. "Just for a few hours."

Her laughter followed her into the kitchen, and Caleb crawled out of bed. He could definitely get used to waking up to the sound of it every morning. He pulled the ring he'd bought for Kourtney out of his bag and stared at it. It was large and flashy, the kind of ring Kourtney would've liked. But it didn't fit Alex. She'd like something plain and simple.

He snapped the jewelry box closed and stuffed it back in his bag. It was way too soon to be thinking about marriage proposals. First, he needed to see where things went with them now that he was home. If the last few days were any indication, though, he could see himself spending his future with Alex.

Caleb hopped in for a quick shower. After he got dressed, he found a sticky note on the front of the coffeemaker. *I'm downstairs if you need me.*

He looked at the no-nonsense scrawl and grinned. No hearts. No flowers. Just the essentials. He poured a cup of coffee and went down to the garage. The front doors were open, and several cars waited on the lifts, but not a soul was inside. A laugh came from the sidewalk outside and drew him there.

It seemed like the entire town had gathered along Main Street. Caleb hung back, watching the citizens chatting with each other over their morning coffee and catching up on the local news. A group with several people he recognized from his brief stay in town had formed near the garage. Miss Martha, the B&B owner. Miss Ada from the café. Earl from the bar. And in the heart of it was Alex. She beamed at her neighbors, completely relaxed and yet shining so brightly in her element that his breath hitched.

How could I have not seen her before?

He inched closer to the sidewalk, not wanting to interrupt the conversation, but still wanting to listen in.

He'd gotten so absorbed listening that he never heard someone approaching him. A hand landed on his shoulder, and he jumped.

"Careful," J.T. said, steadying Caleb's coffee mug. The sunlight flashed on his police badge. "Wouldn't want to charge me with assault after you got burned."

"Sorry—didn't see you." He took a sip of the coffee and waited for his pulse to drop down a notch. "Is it always like this in the morning?"

"Just about. The whole town loves Alex."

"I can see why."

"It's because she loves this town as much as her dad did. We all do. Me, Bubba, Lisa—we all could've left and gone someplace else, but there's something about being home, you know?"

Caleb gave J.T. a tight smile and tried to imagine his old neighborhood in Chicago being like this. "That's one of the sacrifices of being in the Air Force, though. I'm always having to PCS to the next base."

"Yeah, I got a taste of that in the Army. Didn't suit me." J.T.'s face grew serious. "I don't think it would suit Alex, either."

A chill raced down Caleb's spine, making his hair stand on end. "Meaning?"

"Just that. I like you and all—you seem like a great guy—but I also know Alex, and she'll never leave this town. So before you let things go too far, just remember she's not the type of girl who'd make a good military wife."

His throat tightened. It was the same reason Kourtney had given him. "Thanks for the warning."

"Hey, you Air Force guys have your heads in the clouds so much, it takes some of us Army guys to bring you back down to earth." J.T. gave him a light smack on the shoulder before joining the conversation with Alex and the other small business owners.

He finished his coffee and disappeared upstairs as the crowd started dispersing to open up their shops along Main Street. The lively, high-pitched whirl of the machines below marked the start of the workday in the garage, but his mood remained somber. A shield of ice surrounded his heart.

Was he just fooling himself to think he had a future with Alex? Or would she end things with him for the same reason her sister had?

And if she did, would he be willing to let her go?

Or was he better off ending things first?

****

When Alex came upstairs to get cleaned up after work, she'd half expected Caleb to follow her into the shower like he'd done yesterday. But when she emerged from the bathroom, he was still in the same place she'd left him— on the couch with his eyes glued to the video game he was playing.

At least he was dressed for the rehearsal dinner party. He wore the same sport coat from the night in Atlanta, but he'd toned it down with a pair of jeans and a crisp, button-down shirt that matched his bright blue eyes. The result was sophisticated, but sexy as hell.

She leaned over and placed a kiss on his cheek. "I'll be ready in a few minutes."

"Okay," he replied in a flat voice, his attention never

158

leaving the game.

A chill rippled down her spine and shook her very core. This wasn't the same Caleb from this morning who didn't want to leave her bed. It was like a stranger had come and taken over his body. She backed away, holding on the towel wrapped around her for dear life. "Is something wrong?"

"Nope. Just waiting on you."

Her gut tightened, and warning bells rang in the back of her mind. Something had changed, and she had no idea why.

She retreated to her bedroom and put on the same dress and heels she'd worn two nights ago. That got his attention last time. A few minutes later, she came out and announced, "I'm ready."

He finally turned from the game. His face remained blank as he looked at her, but there was no hiding the heat in his eyes. He still wanted her, but everything else about him had reverted to indifference. He set the controller aside and stood. "Let's go, then."

She fought to keep her pain hidden. "Fine. We'll take my truck."

He followed a good three feet behind her, never touching, never saying a word as he climbed into the truck. When they started driving, he stared out the window, his back to her.

Alex wrung her damp palms along the steering wheel. She waited until they were on the outskirts of town before tension became more than she could bear. "Damn it, Caleb, what the hell is wrong with you?"

"What do you mean?"

"I mean, you couldn't keep your hands off of me this morning, and now you're acting like you want nothing to do with me."

He continued to stare out the window. His shoulders rose and fell with a heavy sigh. "I just had some time to think about things today, that's all."

"And?"

Several beats of silence hung in the air before he said, "This week has been fun and all, Alex, but do we really have a future together?"

His question slammed into her as though she'd just crashed her truck into a tree. Her vision blurred with stinging tears that she refused to let fall. So that was it, huh? A week of fun. A rebound romance—that's all she was to him. And she should've seen it coming. Hell, she'd even told him she'd loved him, but he never returned to sentiment.

She swallowed her grief and let her pride take over. "Fine, but you agreed to be my date for the wedding, so don't back out on me now."

"I won't." He went back to staring out the window, oblivious to the agony his words had just caused.

She drove on, grateful to have those extra miles to pull herself together by the time they arrived at the McClures' home. She should've known better than to give Caleb her heart, but she would keep her end of the bargain, too. She would let him go once the wedding was over and try to forget how close to perfect her life had almost been.

****

There had to be a special place in hell for assholes like him.

Caleb longed to hold Alex in his arms and apologize for being such a dick, but his mind held him back. He was doing this for her own good. For his own good, too. There was no need to continue this relationship any further when it would just hit the same dead end.

That still didn't ease the pain in the center of his chest.

He cast a sideways glance at her. Her bottom lip jutted out ever so slightly, softening the hard lines of her clenched jaw. Her eyes glistened with unshed tears.

Shit!

He knew his behavior would hurt her, but he hated watching her try to be so brave when she was probably dying inside like he was. The sad part was, until J.T. had pointed out her ties to Jackson Grove, he'd actually thought there might be a chance for them. But the more he thought about it, the more he saw the truth for what it was. Alex could've gone anywhere with her degree, but she chose to return home and open up a garage. If that wasn't the evidence he needed that she'd never leave this place to follow him, he didn't know what was.

More important, he didn't want to ask her to leave. He'd seen how much the town meant to her and how much she meant to the town. If he forced her to give it all up and move in with him, she'd probably just end up resenting him and leaving him just like Kourtney had done.

He stretched his legs out and pushed his doubts deeper into his gut. Yes, he was doing the right thing, no matter how much it killed him.

They pulled into the crowded horseshoe-shaped driveway of a plantation-style home that rivaled Alex's mother's. Alex found a place to park and hopped out of the truck as soon as she killed the engine. She was halfway to the house before he caught up to her.

"Alex, wait, I thought I was supposed to be your date."

"You're welcome to stay in the truck, if you want."

"That's not what I want."

She spun around on those sexy heels and wobbled, falling into his outstretched arms. For a split second, everything seemed as it should be. He was holding her, the curves of her body pressing against him and reminding them how well they fit together. Then she reminded him that things weren't perfect anymore by pushing him away. "Then what the hell do you want?"

You.

But the answer never made it out of his mind. He forced his mouth closed, unable to tell her the truth without the risk of hurting her even more. "I want to keep my end of our bargain."

She pinched the bridge of her nose. "Let's just be quick about this, then. Make an appearance, maybe grab a bite, and then get the hell out of here."

She walked ahead of him, giving him a nice view of how her ass wiggled in that tight silvery dress. His dick hardened as his vision swept down to take in her long legs and those heels that screamed sex. The idea of hauling her back to the truck and burying himself inside her crossed his mind.

He curled his hands into fists. *I need a drink before I completely lose it.*

Caleb closed the gap between them by the time she reached the front door so when it opened, they appeared to be a happy couple. Alex looped her arm through his and fixed a smile on her face, acting like nothing was wrong as she greeted the people she knew inside. She introduced him as her date for the wedding over and over again, never referring to him as her boyfriend or something more than just an escort for the weekend.

He was fine with it all until he caught the appreciative glances she was getting from the other men at the party. He wasn't the only one admiring how well the strapless dress fit her or how those heels made her legs seem to go on forever. He edged closer to her, finally shifting his position until he stood behind her with a possessive arm around wrapped around her waist. Things might be over for them after tomorrow, but for tonight, she was his.

They worked their way back to the cooler in the kitchen and grabbed a couple of beers. Alex studied him over the rim of her longneck. "You know, you are probably the most frustrating and irritating man I know."

"Thanks for the compliment." He took a long sip, hoping it would ease his rattled nerves. He'd rather take on a combat mission than deal with the conflicting emotions warring inside him right now.

"Funny—I meant it as an insult." She came closer and dropped her voice to a whisper. "I want to know the truth, Caleb. What happened between this morning and now? Did my sister call you?"

"No."

"Did I suddenly turn into an old hag?"

He risked running his gaze over once again, desire heating his blood by the time he made it back to her face. "No."

"Then what?"

A loud laugh by the pool drew his attention to J.T. Her friend's warning about Alex never leaving this town steeled his commitment to ending things with Alex before they got too involved.

She followed his eyes and scowled. "Excuse me for a moment."

Alex stormed out to the pool and yanked J.T. from the group. The windows buffered the heated conversation between them, but the flash in her eyes told him that she had put two and two together. When she came back in, her cheeks were flushed. She took Caleb's hand in a tight hold that left no room for argument and led him away from the crowd to a side hallway.

"Where are we going?"

"This way."

She led him through the house like they were two kids trying to sneak past their parents and stopped at a closed door at the end of a hall. She reached up to the top of the frame and felt around. "There should be a key up here."

"How do you know that?"

"Because this is where the McClures keep their liquor, and Bonnie and I used to sneak in here all the time to steal a sip or two." She paused and grinned as she showed him the key. "Here it is."

"Who's Bonnie?"

"Ryan's little sister. She was part of my gang of friends back in high school, but she left town after we graduated." She fit the key into the lock and opened the door to reveal a room with a pool table and a small bar. "Her parents didn't approve of her 'lifestyle.'"

He wanted to find out more about Alex's friend since it seemed like a safer topic than imagining what they could do in a locked room, but once the door closed behind them, Alex wrapped her arms around his neck and guided his lips toward hers. "Here's a piece of friendly advice— J.T. is full of shit."

Even though it wasn't the first time Alex had ambushed him with a kiss, it still managed to steal his breath away. This time, however, a hint of anger lashed out in the flicks of her tongue and the press of her fingertips. Alex didn't argue with words, but she still let her mouth do all the talking.

And so far, she was winning the argument. The woman had an art of making him forget about everything but the fire burning between them. He pulled her closer, his hands roaming along the small of her back to the curve of her ass. His cock hardened, begging him to experience her tight warmth one more time. His mind warned him that he was in danger of crossing the line, but his body didn't care. He needed Alex.

Alex ended the kiss, her quick breaths exhaling with a shiver, and held his cheeks in her hands. "Look me in the eye and tell me you don't want me."

Common sense told him to lie to her, but his mind refused to conjure up an excuse. "Alex..." he started, hoping one would come to him soon.

"The truth, Caleb." Alex kissed him again, this time with more seduction and less anger, and he surrendered to the will of his body. He indulged in the sweetness of her mouth, the restrained passion she always offered him, the promise of pure bliss once he was inside her again.

When it seemed like she'd gotten the answer she sought, she ended the kiss. "I don't know what J.T. said to you, but I know what we have is good."

"It's great now, but——"

She shushed him by pressing her finger to his lips. "The future will be there tomorrow, and it's always changing, sometimes due to things beyond our control. All we can do is enjoy this moment that we have together."

His breath caught, intensifying the pounding of his pulse. It was like the same, no-nonsense wisdom she'd given him in her letters. No matter how troubled he was, she'd always known what to say to put his mind at ease, even now. "You're right, Alex. We just have this moment."

She pulled his head down to whisper in his ear. "By the way, I'm not wearing any underwear."

All the blood abandoned his brain and went straight for his crotch. "You shouldn't have said that."

She gave him a sexy laugh. "Care to do something about it?"

This was his chance to push her away and politely tell her that he felt guilty for taking advantage of her when he knew there was no hope of a future between them, but he couldn't deny the hunger pulsating through his body. He couldn't resist what she offered, what he needed, what he fully intended to savor as long as he could. He didn't know what tomorrow or the next day held, but he would follow her advice and enjoy the present.

He backed her up to the pool table and sat her on the edge. This time, he initiated the kiss, letting her know in no uncertain terms how crazy she made him.

She didn't shrink away or urge him to slow down. Instead, she devoured him in the same manner. She yanked his jacket off and tugged his shirt out, slowly undressing him while never breaking the rhythm of their kiss. She spread her legs apart and pulled him closer to where he could feel her heat through the thick denim of his jeans.

It was almost more than he could bear. His balls tightened. He needed to get inside her now. His hands traveled up her thighs, confirming what she'd teased him with earlier. He pressed his fingers inside the slick folds, finding that tiny nub that made her moan with pleasure every time he grazed it.

"Caleb." She said his name like a dying plea and unzipped his jeans.

"There's a condom in my wallet," he managed to say, forcing himself to stay out of her until she retrieved it and put it on. Once he had protection in place, he plunged into her and almost came right there.

She wrapped her legs around his waist, the angle allowing him to go even deeper than before. "Damn, you feel so good."

"The feeling is mutual." He started moving inside her like a desperate man. Hard. Fast. Deep. Holding nothing back. This wasn't the time and place for leisurely lovemaking. This was all about the release, about making her come as hard as he knew he would.

It didn't take long. Her walls clenched around his cock, and her body stiffened. He managed to smother her cry of joy with a kiss and rammed into her one more time before his own rush of pleasure overcame him. The force of the orgasm whooshed the air from his lungs and blurred the edges of his consciousness. Black spots danced in front of his eyes. His heart beat wildly, practically singing her name with each throb. His body spasmed with each wave of bliss that rolled through him. She'd claimed him—body, heart, and soul—and he was willing to fight to keep her now.

When he came back down to earth, he was surprised he was standing. Alex's legs were still around his waist, bracing him and keeping him from sliding into a puddle on the floor. He gulped in a few breaths and looked into her eyes. A sense of awe filled him. He was one lucky son of a bitch to have a woman like Alex, and he thankfully had two more days to be by her side.

She ran her fingers through his hair. "See? We are good together."

He nodded, not trusting what would come out of his mouth. He was falling more and more in love with her, but the fresh wounds on his heart kept him from telling her that. Until he knew what would become of them after Sunday, he needed to guard his heart from any more damage.

He pushed off the pool table and disposed of the condom in the wastebasket. "We should probably head back to the party before people notice we're missing."

She hopped off the table and tugged down her dress. "Yeah, I suppose we could make a few more obligatory rounds before heading home and going back to bed." Her voice hinted that she was eager to do more than just sleep once they got to her place.

And God help him, he hoped he had the stamina to

satisfy her.

She unlocked the door and opened it, startling a kissing Kourtney and Ryan on the other side. Alex grinned and handed them the key. "It's all yours."

Caleb stifled his laughter, noting that he didn't feel a shard of jealousy at seeing his ex in the arms of another man.

He took Alex's hand and led her back to the party, leaving his past with Kourtney far behind him. From now on, his future revolved around the one woman who knew his heart better than he did.

CHAPTER THIRTEEN

Alex laid her head on Caleb's shoulder and swayed to the soft Hawaiian music. The scent of the citronella tiki torches filled the air, and the drone of dozens of conversations surrounded her. Lightning bugs flickered across the backyard as twilight darkened the sky. She drew it all in and smiled. She and Caleb had hit a speed bump this afternoon, but now they were back to where they belonged—in each other's arms.

"So what is with the luau theme?" he asked.

"Kourtney and Ryan are going to Hawaii for their honeymoon."

"Ah, I see." He squeezed his arms around her waist, pressing her body against his. "Are you ready for one of those frou-frou drinks with the umbrellas?"

"I'm happy right where I am." But the growl that rippled through her stomach reminded her that she'd skipped lunch to finish fixing that fuel pump before the garage closed.

Caleb chuckled and took a step back. "I think that's my cue to get you something to eat."

"Fine. I'll grab us some seats by the pool." She placed a quick kiss on his cheek and watched him disappear into the house.

A few seconds later, her sister appeared from the same doorway and marched toward her, eyes dark with fury. "Alexandra Louise Leadbetter, I need to have a word with you right now."

Uh-oh. It was always bad news whenever her mother or her sister used her full name.

Kourtney grabbed her upper arm and hauled her to the back corner of the pool where there were fewer people. "What on earth possessed you to defile the McClures' gaming room like that?"

"It's not like you and Ryan weren't heading there for the exact same reason."

Kourtney's cheeks turned red, and she glanced around to see if anyone overheard her. "You could have at least covered up what you were doing," she said in a sharp whisper, "not leaving the condom wrapper on the middle of the table."

"Sorry, but we were kind of caught up in the moment."

Kourtney's nostrils flared, and her cheeks grew as red as her lipstick. She poked her finger into the center of Alex's chest with enough force to make her stumble back. "I know what you're trying to do. You're determined to ruin my wedding, and I won't stand for it."

"Will you quit with the crazy accusation?"

"It's the truth." Another jab of her finger forced Alex back even more. "It's time you think about the repercussions of your actions and how they reflect on our family."

"And it's time you got your head out of your ass and realize that I'm never going to be like you and Mama."

"No, you're just my horrid little sister who's done

nothing but embarrass me all my life."

Kourtney ended her tirade with her hardest jab yet, and Alex stumbled back once again, her ankle twisting. The heel of her shoe fell over the edge of the pool. She wobbled, her hands flying out to catch nothing but air. Kourtney's face morphed from anger to wide-mouthed shock as Alex fell backward. A solid *thwack* against the back of her head was the last thing she remembered before the blackness surrounded her.

****

Caleb returned from the kitchen with a plateful of food and groaned at the thick wall of people staring at something on the other end of the pool. By the time he pushed his way to the front, he saw what had captured their attention.

Kourtney appeared to be ripping Alex to shreds with a tirade, pushing her younger sister closer to the edge of the pool with every other word. A shout of warning formed on his lips with the final push. Alex's shoe hit the lip of the pool surround, and she fell back.

Time stood still. He dropped the plate and rushed toward her, but he could've been swimming in sand for as fast as he seemed to be moving.

Her head connected with the diving board with a loud *bang* that snapped her neck forward. His pulse jumped into his throat. *Oh God, oh God, oh God...*

Alex hit the water with a loud splash. A cloud of red marked where she'd fallen into the pool, but she never resurfaced.

Caleb dived in after her. The water was a fog of blood and bubbles when he opened his eyes to look for her.

Another shadow swam toward the limp body sinking to the bottom. Caleb kicked toward her, reaching her the same time J.T. did.

Her best friend braced her neck and nodded to Caleb, pushing off the floor of the pool to bring Alex up. His lungs burned from holding his breath, but even after he gulped the air when they broke the surface, the ache remained.

Alex was unconscious, her lips blue and her face deathly pale.

A sob formed in the center of his chest. *Oh God, oh God, oh God.*

"Keep her steady," J.T. warned, bringing him back to reality. "She could have a spinal injury."

Caleb nodded, supporting her back as J.T. led them to the shallow end of the pool. His pilot training had included instruction on water rescues, but he'd never dreamed he'd be using it on the woman he loved. "Someone get us a stiff board," he shouted, his eyes never leaving her face.

Breathe, damn it! Breathe!

But Alex's chest didn't move.

Blood swirled around them from the wound on the back of her head. Someone collapsed one of the folding tables the guests had been eating on and lowered it into the water. It wasn't a proper backboard, but it would work. J.T. continued to hold her neck perfectly still as they floated her onto it and pulled her out of the water.

The distant wail of a siren floated on the breeze, growing louder with each passing second, but it was still too far away to do any good. Alex still hadn't taken a breath.

"She still has a weak pulse," J.T. said from her head, his finger over the artery in her neck.

Caleb swallowed back his fear and let his instincts take over. *Not breathing, but still has a pulse. No chest compressions needed, but she still needs rescue breaths.* He thrust her jaw up and pinched her nose while taking a deep breath. Then he covered her mouth with his own and forced air into her water-logged lungs.

Nothing happened.

He repeated the same actions over and over again, his gut tightening with each breath.

Please don't die on me, Alex. Please don't die. I love you.

The force of his realization rocked him to the core and paralyzed him. He loved her. He loved her, and he'd been too chicken-shit to tell her when he had a chance.

"Caleb!"

J.T.'s sharp command jerked him back, and he gave Alex another breath.

This time, a deep cough rattled through her chest and jerked her limp body. Caleb lifted the edge of the table to help roll her to the side, making sure her spine was still kept in alignment. A gush of water poured from her mouth, followed by the most wonderful sound in the world—a sharp gasp.

Alex continued to cough, forcing more water out with each spasm that rocked her body before taking in another breath.

The medics arrived on the scene and pushed him away. By the time they'd transferred her to a backboard, she was taking shallow breaths on her own. Her lips were still blue under the oxygen mask they'd placed on her and blood continued to soak through the bandage they were hastily wrapping around her head, but she was alive.

The only thing that kept him from being fully relieved was that she never opened her eyes.

In a matter of minutes, the medics had her strapped to a stretcher. The sirens blared with an ear-bursting screech, and the ambulance took off with Alex in the back.

J.T. put his hand on Caleb's shoulder and beckoned him toward the police car at the end of the driveway. "I know this borders on abusing my authority, especially when I'm off duty…"

"Just do it."

J.T. turned on his car's sirens and took off in pursuit of the ambulance. They arrived at the hospital just as the medics were unloading Alex.

Her eyes met his, and relief rushed through Caleb's veins with enough force to make his knees buckle. He grabbed the edge of the police car and fought back the tears that threatened to spill out. Maybe she would pull though this. Maybe he would be given a second chance to make things right.

Alex disappeared into the ER, and he was left with knots of worry in his stomach. Kourtney and Ryan showed up, followed by Bubba and Lisa, and finally, Alex's mother.

Mrs. Leadbetter didn't bother to linger in the waiting room like the others. Instead, she barged right through the ER doors, her voice as loud as a drill sergeant's. "Alexandra Louise Leadbetter, where are you?"

Caleb rushed after her. A nurse tried to intercept her,

but the arrogant matriarch shoved her aside. "I'm not leaving until I see her."

He held out hope that Alex's mom was worried about her daughter's health until she said, "As soon as she's able to speak, she needs to apologize to me and her sister and the McClures for ruining the rehearsal dinner."

Something inside him snapped. "How dare you think about only yourself at a time like this?" He stood in front of Mrs. Leadbetter, his fists clenched tightly at his sides to keep from striking her. "Alex almost died because Kourtney *pushed* her into the pool, and you have the gall to demand Alex apologize?"

Then, to his surprise, Kourtney appeared at his side. "He's right, Mama. Alex did nothing wrong."

Mrs. Leadbetter's mouth hung open in shock.

Kourtney wrapped her arm around her mother's shoulders and led her back to the waiting room, her calm words a stark contrast to his angry outburst. "Now, let's leave Alex alone long enough to let the doctors take care of her."

Disgust rolled through his stomach at he took a seat in the deserted island of chairs in the middle of the room. How could a mother be so heartless when it came to her daughter? It made him want to kidnap Alex and take her far away from her fucked-up, self-centered family. Why would she want to stay in the same town as a mother who obviously despised her?

And yet, when he looked around the room, he saw plenty of people who cared about Alex. They were fractured off into separate groups, all there for the same person.

It was Kourtney who finally broke the ice. She sat down in the chair next to him, staring straight ahead as she spoke. "I never should've let my temper get the better of me like that."

"No shit."

"Damn it, Caleb, I'm just as worried as you are, maybe more."

"Why? Because you could be facing manslaughter charges if she dies? Talk about ruining your wedding."

"I'm being serious here."

"So am I." He turned to her. "What do you have against Alex, anyway?"

Kourtney clasped her hands in her lap and focused her gaze on them. "Would you believe I'm jealous?"

"Jealous?"

She nodded. "Alex has always been so comfortable being herself. She's smart, generous to a fault, and well-liked by everyone without having to win their affections. Everyone who meets her likes her, and well…" She squirmed in her seat. "I've always had to work to make people like me, and then, I sometimes worry it's just because of how I look."

He mulled over her words, finding truth in each statement. A sinking feeling weighed on his shoulders as he realized he'd been just as guilty as everyone else. He'd fallen for Kourtney's looks and had never bothered to get to really know her before he deployed. He just wanted to possess her and make the rest of the guys in his unit jealous. It wasn't until he got those emails that he came to value the woman within.

Only it wasn't Kourtney he'd fallen in love with. It was

the woman who'd nearly died this afternoon. The woman he'd never really noticed until this week. The woman who had no idea how much he loved her.

"What about him?" he asked, nodding toward Ryan.

A wan smile formed on her lips. "He gets me, and he makes me a better person."

"Then I wish you every happiness with him."

"I wish the same for you and Alex, even though I know it won't be easy."

Her statement carried the same warning J.T.'s had. Alex was too tied to the town. She'd never leave.

He curled his fingers into his palms. Maybe not, but he'd try his best to convince her to give this relationship at chance.

A doctor appeared from the ER, and everyone gathered around him. Caleb lingered toward the back, the obvious outsider. Everyone else had known Alex her entire life. But Lisa looped her arm through his and pulled him to the front as the doctor started to speak. The words blurred together. Concussion. Laceration. Needing oxygen. Keeping overnight. But at the very end, he heard the words he'd longed to hear from the moment he saw her fall.

"She should pull through this and be backing to fixing cars in a few days."

He released a shaky breath. Alex was going to be okay.

"She's a bit tuckered out from all the excitement," the doctor continued, "so don't all rush her at once. Just a few of you at a time once we get her to a room."

The group broke up again, Kourtney leading Ryan and her mother off into one corner while Lisa led him away to

Bubba and J.T.

"I'm glad she's going to be all right," Lisa said. "From what Doc Murphy said, it could've been much worse, but we all know Alex is tougher than she looks."

The men nodded, and J.T. added, "But I'm definitely giving her a hard time when she gets home for that minor heart attack she gave me."

"You and me both," Caleb agreed with a weak smile. "Thanks for rescuing her."

"Hey, it was a team effort." J.T. gave him a playful smack on the arm. "I couldn't have done it without you."

"It looks like folks are heading home." Bubba nodded to Alex's mom and Ryan as they were walking out the door. "Sounds like we should head home, too, and visit Alex in the morning."

The others nodded and left him alone with Kourtney in the waiting room.

The gap between them seemed wider than the physical space. They'd both moved on, but some of the post-breakup awkwardness remained.

Kourtney ran her thumb along the strap of her purse. "Do you mind if I go up and see her first? I really need to get back to the party and…" She choked. "And I need to apologize to her."

The old Kourtney would've left once she knew Alex was fine, needing to resume her position as the center of attention. But this Kourtney wanted to make things right before she left. Maybe Ryan was turning her into a better person, after all. "Go ahead. I'll stay with her tonight and call you if anything changes."

"Thanks." She rang for the elevator and disappeared

behind the sliding doors.

Caleb sank back into his chair, welcoming the few extra moments to gather his thoughts. Kourtney wasn't the only one who needed to apologize to Alex, and he hoped by the time morning rolled around, Alex would know the contents of his heart.

CHAPTER FOURTEEN

Alex tugged at the uncomfortable plastic mask around her nose and mouth. The oxygen flowing through it had a sterile, medicinal smell to her that reminded her with every breath that she was a patient.

She pulled the covers around her shoulders and shivered, aggravating the pain in her chest and the pounding in the back of her skull. A cough only added to the agony. She turned to the nurse who was still fussing with all the equipment strapped to Alex. "Can I at least have a Tylenol?"

"I'll go ask the doctor," she replied and left the room.

Alex rolled her eyes back and sank deeper into her pillows. Maybe in a few hours, she'd get her Tylenol. Doc Murphy already warned he couldn't give her any strong pain medication due to her head injury.

What a crappy way to end the day. She'd been looking forward to enjoying another night in Caleb's arms before he had to leave, and now this happened. The worst part was, she couldn't remember exactly what had happened. The last thing she remembered was getting reamed by her sister.

A soft knock came from the doorway.

Speak of the devil…

Kourtney stood there, her eyes lowered. "May I come in?"

Alex nodded, offering a silent prayer she wouldn't get screamed at for ruining the rehearsal dinner.

Kourtney pulled the lone chair up to the edge of the bed and sat down. A sniffle started the flow of tears, followed by an outright sob. "I'm so sorry, Alex," she blubbered.

Alex grabbed the tissue box and handed it to her sister. "For what?"

"For pushing you into the pool. I don't know what came over me. I was just so angry and jealous and..." She paused to blow her nose and wipe away the mascara streaming down her cheeks. "I never meant to hurt you. You're my baby sister, after all."

Alex dug her fingers into her blanket, scared to move. *Did an alien come and take over my sister's body while I was out?*

"Please forgive me, Alex. I promise I won't be so horrid. I promise to try to be a better sister." Kourtney laced her fingers through Alex's. "Just please forgive me."

"Even though I've ruined your wedding, just like you always said I would?"

A laugh mixed with a sob, reviving the black-tinged trail of tears on her sister's cheeks. "I'm the one who ruined it, not you. You haven't done anything wrong. It's all my fault."

Humility was never one of Kourtney's virtues, which made the scene in front of her even more strange. But it seemed genuine. Alex squeezed her sister's hand and said, "It's okay, Kourtney. I forgive you."

The sobbing ceased for a second. "You do?"

Alex nodded. "If it makes you feel any better, I don't even remember exactly what happened."

That triggered a new wave of crying that took Kourtney the better part of a minute to control. "I've been so petty and selfish this past week, especially when it came to you and Caleb. I've found someone who makes me happy, and I should've been glad to see that you did the same for him, but I was just so jealous. I saw how he looked at you." She fumbled with the wet, wadded tissue in her hand. "He never looked that way at me."

"But what about your warning about him breaking my heart?"

"Maybe I spoke too soon. After all, the choice is yours."

A shiver of dread raced down her spine, and Alex buried herself deeper under the covers. What would she choose? Would she be willing to give up her life in Jackson Grove to be with Caleb?

She pushed those thoughts out of her mind. "So, if I push the doc to let me go tomorrow morning, maybe I can get out in time to make it to the wedding."

Kourtney gave her a sisterly smile, still holding on to her hand. "I'd like for you to be there, but if you can't, I understand that it's nobody's fault but my own."

Alex tilted her head to the side. It was the second time Kourtney had admitted she was in the wrong. "Who are you, and what have you done with my sister?"

Kourtney lowered her eyes and laughed. "Let's just say Ryan helped me put things in perspective on the way over here. He's good at that, you know."

"Then it sounds like you've found a good man."

"I have. Ryan and me, we've always tried to keep things casual, but when I came home and he was there for me, I knew I couldn't live without him. And once we both realized we felt the same way about each other, we saw no reason to wait any longer. Hell, I would've gone to the courthouse and married him the day after he proposed if Mama hadn't insisted on the big wedding."

A lump formed in Alex's throat. It was like she was talking with a perfect stranger. She'd always been so ready to dismiss Kourtney as selfish and superficial that she'd never really gone out of her way to get to know the woman underneath. "I'm sorry, too."

"For what?"

"For being the selfish one and trying to make Caleb fall in love with me."

Kourtney patted her hand. "You didn't have to try very hard if my observations are correct. The boy just needed to open his eyes."

"Do you think we can start over? Try to be real sisters instead of what we've spent most of our lives being?"

Kourtney pressed her lips together and nodded. "I think that sounds like a superb idea."

The last bit of angst fled, and Alex's eyelids grew heavy. "Is Caleb still here?"

"He's downstairs waiting for me to finish." Kourtney stood and checked her reflection in the mirror. "Oh, holy hell! I look like an extra from that TV show about zombies."

Alex chuckled as her sister opened up her purse and started to fix the ruined makeup. This might take a while. She gave into her weariness and closed her eyes.

When she opened them again, Caleb was at her side. She gave him a weak smile. "How long was I asleep?"

"About an hour." He pulled the chair closer. "How are you feeling?"

"Can I get back to you in a bit?"

He brushed back a strand of her unruly hair. "You're not going to complain just a little bit?"

"Complaining doesn't fix anything."

A grin flashed across his face before it fell back into a somber expression. "I realized something today, Alex."

Her pulse quickened. Was this where he told her that he was leaving and that things were over between them? She licked her dry lips. "What's that?"

"I love you."

Her heart skipped a couple of beats before going full throttle on her. "You love me?"

He nodded, still brushing her hair. "I was trying to play it safe this afternoon, especially after J.T. told me you'd never leave this town to follow me. I was too scared he was right and I'd end up getting my heart broken again, but this afternoon…" He glanced to the side and took a deep breath. "This afternoon, I realized how much you mean to me, and I want to tell you every minute of every day that I love you."

"Wouldn't that get monotonous after a while?" she teased, despite the growing tightness in her chest. "I love you, too."

He leaned over and brushed a kiss on her temple. "You were right, you know. We can't think about tomorrow, especially when something could come along and take it away from us. We can just enjoy what we have now."

"You're right." She pushed the thoughts of what would happen after Sunday to the corner of her mind. "We just have now."

"And thank my lucky stars that you hacked your sister's email so you could deceive me because if you hadn't, I would've never gotten to know how wonderful you really are."

"So you forgive me for tricking you into falling in love with me?"

"Does this answer your question?" He pulled her oxygen mask to the side and kissed her until the monitor next to the bed started bleeping. "We'd better stop before the nurses rush in here and catch us."

"Let them." She pulled him closer for one more kiss.

Chapter Fifteen

A few weeks later

Caleb ran his finger along the bow tie around his neck and wished for the ninetieth time that day he'd chosen to wear his mess dress. But this was Adam's wedding, not his, and he wore the same tuxedoes as the rest of his brothers instead of his formal Air Force uniform.

The seven of them were gathered outside the church for photos before the wedding. The late spring day promised to be warm and sunny, with a cool breeze blowing in off Lake Michigan. It was a perfect day for a wedding, and he relished the chance to spend time with his brothers in one location. Over a year had passed since they'd all managed to come home for Christmas before he deployed, but it was like no time had passed once they were together.

Frank came up and gave him a playful tackle of a hug. "Hey, where's that hot redhead of yours?"

"She couldn't make it," he replied with a tight smile. "Said she had a last-minute emergency at the garage."

Up until yesterday morning, though, he'd fully expected Alex to be his date for the wedding. When he'd left Jackson Grove a few weeks ago, they'd made a promise to make their relationship work, despite the distance. Every

187

day, they'd talk on the phone or exchange emails. As always, she knew just what to say to make him fall even deeper in love with her. He'd been counting down the hours until he could hold her again and offer the ring he'd bought for her, but her phone call last night had killed his anticipation with a full-force blow to the gut.

"Tough break, bro. I was looking forward to seeing her again, and I know Mom was looking forward to meeting her."

"Yeah, well, shit happens."

He moved back into the group with his brothers, cracking jokes at Adam's expense about being the first one of them to get married, even though Ben was planning on getting married as soon as the Stanley Cup finals were over in a month. The camaraderie distracted him from the ache in his chest. He missed Alex almost to the point of flying down to Alabama after the wedding just so he could see her again and let her know he was ready for his own walk down the aisle.

The low rumble of a classic muscle car jerked him from the conversation. He closed his eyes and savored the sweet sound.

"Wow," Ethan said, "that is one smokin' car."

"Forget the car," Dan countered. "I'll take the driver."

Caleb opened his eyes and peered over his brothers' shoulders. A 1971 orange Roadrunner with black stripes and a retractable air grabber had pulled up in front of the church. The 440 six-pack engine halted, and a tall, slender woman with wild auburn hair and a pair of cowboy boots got out.

His chest tightened, and he blinked several times to

make sure he wasn't dreaming.

"Maybe I should say hello to her," Dan said, but Frank jerked him back.

"No go, bro. She's Caleb's."

"Yeah, you'd need to roll a twenty-one to score with her," Caleb added, referencing the twenty-sided die his twin had carried in his pocket since they were kids. He scrambled down the stairs, his steps slowing as he grew closer.

Alex crossed her arms and leaned back against the car, the wind ruffling her skirt and giving him glimpses of her toned thighs. Her grin widened as he approached.

"What are you doing here?" he asked, still not believing she was here after yesterday's conversation.

"I heard you needed a date for a wedding, so I drove all night to get here in time."

"But the emergency at the garage?"

She bit her bottom lip and glanced down. "Well, it was a little emergency. I was having some reservations about leaving Jermaine in charge for so long and was going to chicken out and…"

"It was only going to be for the weekend, Alex."

"Actually, I was hoping for a bit longer." She moved aside so he could see into her car.

It was packed full.

"I hear Utah's beautiful this time of year," she continued, tripping over some of her words, "and I think it's time I stretch my wings a bit and see what's outside Jackson Grove, maybe see where things go with us." She paused, then added, "That is, if you don't mind me moving in with you for a while."

"Moving in with me?" He looked at the car and back at her. Even after J.T. and Kourtney had warned him Alex would never leave home, he had held onto the hope that maybe they could find a way to be together. He'd even toyed with the idea of resigning his commission, but she'd refused to even let him consider it when he mentioned it to her. And now she was here, packed up and ready to venture to the other side of the country to be with him.

His chest tightened. She'd once told him that love made the impossible possible. Maybe this was her way of showing it.

"No," he said, his voice cracking.

Panic flashed across her face. "No?"

"No, you can't move in with me for a while." He pulled her into his arms. "If you move in with me, I want it to be forever, Alex. You're the last person I want to see before I fall asleep and the first person I want to see when I wake up. You're home to me, no matter where we end up. I want you to be my wife, and I don't want to settle for anything less."

She wound her arms around his neck and smiled. "You can be very demanding, flyboy."

"Only because I never want to lose the best wingman I've ever had." He pressed his lips against hers, cherishing the love and warmth that radiated from her kisses. "So, those are my terms, Hot Wheels. Take it or leave it."

A mischievous glow lit up her whiskey brown eyes as she rolled them off to the side. "Hmm, I might need some more convincing. Those are some pretty stringent terms."

"Now who's the demanding one?" But he kissed her again, this time letting her know in no uncertain terms what three weeks without her had done to his system. His cock grew harder with each flick of her tongue. He reached under her skirt to feel the silkiness of her tights, roving up to discover she'd forgotten her underwear once again. A moan rose from his chest. Dear God, did she have any idea what she did to him?

She responded with a hunger that rivaled his, pressing her body against his and deepening the kiss. Then, just when he was considering moving the Roadrunner to a secluded location where they could finish this, she reached down to give his ass a playful pinch.

He jerked back, his desire doused as she dissolved into laughter. "What was that for?"

"I've been taking lessons from Miss Martha. Besides, I don't want to go about embarrassing you in front of your family. This is your brother's wedding, after all."

"But after the reception?"

"I'm all yours." She ran her finger along the lapels of his jacket. "And to answer your offer, I'm okay with forever as long as I have you. Like you said—with you, I'm home."

"You'll always have me. I lost my heart to you long before I realized you were the one who'd stolen it." He placed a chaste kiss on her forehead, not wanting to risk any teasing from his brothers for the hard-on she'd give him if he kissed her the way he wanted to. "Would you like to meet my family?"

"I'd like that very much."

"Good, because I know they'll love you as much as I do."

He kept his arm around her waist as he turned around

and led her up the stairs where his mother had joined his brothers. Unlike the time he'd introduced Kourtney to his mom, he had no jitters, no hesitations, no sick nervous feeling in his stomach. His chest swelled with pride as he gazed down at the woman who'd just agreed to spend forever with him. This was love. This was real. And this was the impossible made possible.

His lucky charm pressed against his thigh, but he didn't need to rub it. He already was the luckiest man in the world. "Mom, guys, I'd like you to meet my fiancée, Alex."

A Note to Readers

Dear Reader,

Thank you so much for reading *Falling for the Wingman*. I hope you enjoyed it and look forward to the next book in the series, *The Heart's Game*. If you did, please leave a review at the store where you bought this book or on Goodreads.

I love to hear from readers. You can find me on Facebook and Twitter, or you can email me using the contact form on my website, www.CristaMcHugh.com.

If you would like to be the first to know about new releases or be entered into exclusive contests, please sign up for my newsletter using the contact form on my website.

Also, please like my Facebook page for more excerpts and teasers from upcoming books. And, just for this series, I have a special website featuring more information on the Kelly Brothers, playlists, recipes, and other extras just for readers. Please check it out at www.thekellybrothers.cristamchugh.com.

--Crista

Don't miss the next book in the Kelly Brothers series…

THE HEART'S GAME

Robotics engineer Jenny Nguyen has given up on finding Mr. Right. So when her brother and his husband approach her to act as surrogate for their child, she sees it as her only chance to have a child and accepts. One week after she initiates the process, however, she meets a man who gets her heart pumping for all the right reasons and gives into the temptation to spend one night in his arms. When the test turns positive, she's believes she can't handle both the pregnancy and dating, but she underestimates how persistent a Daniel Kelly can be.

When surgeon and gamer-geek Dan meets a pretty woman dressed as a Sailor Scout at a party, a roll of his lucky 20-sided die tells him he should take a gamble on her. One night of passion leaves him longing for more, but Jenny's refusal to return his calls afterward leaves him wondering if the attraction was one-sided. An accidental discovery of her pregnancy has him convinced the baby is his, and he'll stop at nothing to win her heart.

Coming July 2014

Author Bio

Growing up in small town Alabama, Crista relied on storytelling as a natural way for her to pass the time and keep her two younger sisters entertained.

She currently lives in the Audi-filled suburbs of Seattle with her husband and two children, maintaining her alter ego of mild-mannered physician by day while she continues to pursue writing on nights and weekends.

Just for laughs, here are some of the jobs she's had in the past to pay the bills: barista, bartender, sommelier, stagehand, actress, morgue attendant, and autopsy assistant.

And she's also a recovering LARPer. (She blames it on her crazy college days)

For the latest updates, deleted scenes, and answers to any burning questions you have, please check out her webpage, www.CristaMcHugh.com.

Find Crista online at:

Twitter: twitter.com/crista_mchugh

Facebook: www.facebook.com/CristaMcHugh

36657566R00120

Made in the USA
Charleston, SC
09 December 2014